Jou[illegible]
Home

A Novella

Formerly called The Ball

by

Tony Brassell

In memory of all the Channel Island children who were evacuated during World War II

&

Mick Taylor, the Silver Fox, my golfing partner and friend of nearly 40 years who went through the occupation of Guernsey as a child and who died just before I completed this book.

Cover painting by the Author

ISBN: 9798689114569

Introduction

During the 2nd World War, thousands of children from Guernsey and Jersey were evacuated to the United Kingdom. They left in June 1940 and didn't return until the summer or autumn of 1945, five long years later.

Many of the children left with their schools and didn't see their families for all of that time. A few red cross letters were all that kept them in touch.

Children had grown up, made new friends and developed strange accents. Life for them had changed completely.

When they arrived home some parents barely recognised their children, such had been the changes that had taken place as they grew up during those 5 years of absence. Some children remembered little about their Island and didn't want to go back to somewhere they no longer called home to be with people they had all but forgotten. These were trying times and it would be many months and years before life would settle down to something approaching normality. Relationships had to be rebuilt as the Channel Islands strove to recover from the occupation which had devastated their economies.

This is the story of two young boys who wanted to get home but because of circumstances beyond their control had been left behind in England. One from Jersey the other from Guernsey, the boys were sporting enemies, but their situation forced them together on a journey neither of them would ever forget.

Take the journey with them as they strive to get home against all the odds and with only one joint passion - football.

The Prologue

In the middle of July 1945, England was starting to recover from almost 6 years of war that had wreaked havoc on the country and its people.

It was the end of term at Taunton School and spirits were high. The war was over, and the Channel Islanders were going home.

The Taunton schoolboys were playing football in their lunch break and amongst the "teams" were a fair smattering of Guernsey and Jersey lads. That always created an edge to any game as the rivalry was as intense here in a playground in Taunton as it was in the Muratti final at either Springfield in Jersey or the Track in Guernsey. (The Muratti Final was the culmination of every domestic football season in the Channel Islands and usually resulted in a match between the two islands, watched by thousands of locals.)

The ball belonged to Peter Cochrane, one of the Guernsey boys, and he always had it with him. It was quite a new leather ball which his adopted family, during his enforced evacuation from Guernsey, had given him for his birthday a few weeks earlier.

As the boys competed and the rare goals were scored in the 20 plus aside match, a good crowd of boys and girls and a few teachers watched and cheered as the game swept up and down the playground.

It was almost time to go back to class when Peter Cochrane, better known as PC, got the ball and sprinted towards the Jersey net. Harold "Harry" Le Maistre from Jersey spotted him and coming at him from his right, launched himself in a last-ditch tackle before PC could shoot at goal. The clash resulted in a crack which could be heard across the school grounds. It was like a shot from a gun. PC's leg took a sickening and unnatural turn and a piece of bone broke the skin and started to bleed. Harry hit the ground like a sack of spuds, his head making contact with the ground and his left arm twisting awkwardly behind him.

PC let out a scream of agony, but Harry never moved. A pool of blood slowly built around his head. Teachers rushed to their aid; one was physically sick at the sight of PC's leg. An ambulance was called and soon both the boys were speeding on their way to hospital to the sound of the ambulance bell. Term had ended early for the lads and they wouldn't be going anywhere for quite some time.

Chapter One

Musgrove Park Hospital in Taunton had been established by the US Army in 1941. It was designed to look after US servicemen injured in the second world war. It was still in use in July 1945 but had started to take a few non army personnel casualties as they had spare beds. With no new casualties coming in, existing patients were gradually being repatriated to the USA as soon as they were fit enough to travel. Due to the nature and seriousness of the boy's injuries the ambulance crew had taken the decision to take them straight to Musgrove as they thought they would be well treated by the experienced American doctors.

The boys were immediately triaged on arrival with PC being taken to the specialist Orthopaedic surgeon while Harry was assessed by a team of specialists including a Neurotrauma specialist and Orthopaedic doctor who assessed his dislocated shoulder. Nurses patched up grazes and cuts on both the boys.

PC was taken to surgery almost immediately and his surgeon, an American Major called Bill Cornelius wasted no time in operating on his leg to repair the broken Tibia and Fibula. As it happened it was a very clean break and didn't need any specialist support. His wound was cleaned, stitched and dressed and then he was taken to a ward with his leg elevated. He would be given a plaster cast later that evening

Harry woke up while his surgeon was assessing him. Colonel Mayweather had seen many head injuries during the war and on first examination wasn't too worried about long term issues for the lad. His shoulder had been pulled back into place before he came around but he also had a broken wrist so that was reset and supported until the plaster technician was available to work his magic. He had received a nasty cut to his head which was stitched and bandaged while he was unconscious but there appeared to be no swelling and he was quite responsive when he awoke. As a precaution his arm was placed in a supported sling and he was ordered to rest for some time until the Doctor was sure there was no internal damage to his head which could worsen if he moved around too much.

With that he was wheeled to the same ward and put in a bed next to PC. After all they were from the same school so must be friends. How wrong could they be!!

PC was in the last bed of the pristine, white painted, hospital ward. There were 12 beds in all and his was in the corner giving him a view out of one of the windows. From there he could see the grounds and, beyond some roof tops, the countryside which was easily visible despite their ground floor vantage point. Harry was slotted into the 11th bed in the row and a curtain was drawn to separate the boys from the men in the rest of the ward. Nurses, in their immaculate uniforms and small white hats fussed around them to make sure they were comfortable and had everything they needed. Their clothes were placed in lockers by the side of each bed and they were asked if they wanted anything to eat for their supper.

Both ordered fish, boiled potatoes and vegetables and glasses of milk but the coincidence didn't raise a smile as neither boy felt like talking to the other.

Before tea arrived one of the teachers from Taunton School came to see them and see how they were. She brought each boy a kit-bag with a few more clothes, some books for them to read and PC's football that they had been playing with, signed by their teachers and some of their friends as a get-well message.

She spoke to the Doctors for a while and then turned to leave. But before she left, she stopped and turned to the boys.

'Look after each other boys,' she said, 'you may be here for some time.'

With that she headed off and they were on their own. Nothing was said.

About 15 minutes later their tea arrived, and the nurses tried to make them as comfortable as possible so they could eat their meals. The nurses were all smiles and so nice the boys could not help but engage with them and chat, but they resolutely ignored each other. Sister Christine came to check on them while they were eating. They knew straight away that she was in charge as the other nurses scurried away when she arrived. Looking very sheepish.

'How are you boys?' she asked.

'OK thank you,' replied PC. 'No thanks to that idiot,' he added, pointing at Harry.

'It was an accident.' Harry replied angrily.

'Accident, you deliberately broke my leg.'

'No I didn't!'

'Boys,' Sister Christine interrupted loudly. 'I think you need to get over this. No-one tried to injure anyone, it was just an accident. It happens all the time in sport. You are going to be here for quite a while so if I were you, I would try and make up and be friends. You'll get better much more quickly if you help each other.'

She gave them both a stern look which they knew meant she would take no nonsense from them. They both physically shrank back from that look.

'Are you both friends now?' Sister Christine asked them both.

'Yes miss,' PC replied quietly.

'Sister,' Sister Christine corrected.

'Yes Sister,' they replied in unison.

Sister Christine smiled and turned on her heel. The other nurses who had been watching the exchange nodded, deferentially, stepping back as she passed by them on the way out.

The two boys sat in silence for a while as the nurses went about their business.

The plaster technician came early in the evening and gave them temporary casts as they were going to be assessed again in the morning,

Outside the sun was setting as the day drew to a close. Lights would be out by 10pm but there would still be some faint light in the sky on such a beautiful evening. As with all hospitals, work wouldn't stop, but talking after lights out was not encouraged. As well as the books, the hospital had given them some American comic books. Both were fascinated as they hadn't seen Captain America stories before and those of the Sub Mariner. They were engrossed and during the evening swapped over so they could read further.

They loved them and before the evening was out, they were talking about the characters and stories like long lost pals.

Just before 10pm the nurses came to settle them in and took the comics away. Lights were turned out and both boys lay there looking as the faint light from outside turned to darkness. Both could see the stars from where they lay.

PC turned to Harry and whispered, 'Good night.' Harry smiled back, closed his eyes and went to sleep.

After a good night's sleep, the boys were woken up at 6am sharp to the smell of breakfast. They were given eggs and bacon; Harry being helped with his food and then they were both washed and helped with the toilet. They both were taken for an x-ray on their broken bones to make sure all was OK. This was brand new technology for Taunton and wasn't something the boys had ever heard of before. Once the Doctor was happy that all looked well with how the bones were aligned the plaster technician was called to dress their fractures again. That caused a few muted grunts from both boys as the doctor made sure all was correct before the final plaster was applied. This time they were being brave in front of each other and tried to smile through their discomfort as the vital work was carried out.

Once all was done the Doctor asked how they both felt. PC was happy but Harry mentioned that he had a headache. The Doctor checked his eyes and felt his head and neck. He couldn't spot anything obvious, but the nurses could tell he was concerned as Harry was obviously not happy. Head injuries can get worse after a while and the Doctor was worried about a potential bleed on the brain.

Harry was taken down to the x-ray department and this time his head was strapped to a plate while the x-ray of his skull was taken.

He was taken back to his bed and sedated, so he didn't feel any pain. PC asked if he was OK, but Harry was too sleepy to answer, and the nurses wouldn't tell him anything.

During the rest of the morning the nurses fussed around Harry while PC looked on. For most of the time Harry slept and despite asking several times PC couldn't get anything but smiles and a cup of tea from the nurses. He read more comics to help pass the time and at lunch he enjoyed a hot dog, something else he had never had before. He was starting to enjoy this American way of life.

That afternoon PC was introduced to his pair of crutches. A physiotherapist came in to help him get used to his new friends and show him how to get about by himself. He also gave PC some targets and by the end of week he wanted to see PC outside in the grounds, spending more time out of bed than in.

Harry spent most of the day asleep and during the afternoon his neck was put in a brace to make sure he kept his head as still as possible. They were a right pair, as Sister Christine called them. She sat down with PC at the end of the afternoon and explained that Harry would be kept sedated for another day or two and then they would see if there had been any change in his condition. While she spoke, she sat primly in the chair next to PC's bed.

After tea PC started to feel lonely with no-one to speak to. That didn't last long as his adopted Mum who had looked after him while he had lived in Taunton came to see him.

Glynis had been a great Mum to PC, and he had loved being with her, but he knew that time was coming to an end. He would be going home soon and who knows when he might visit Taunton again.

'Hello Peter love,' she said as she sat down by his bed. 'How's the leg?'

'Not bad Mum,' he replied. He had been told to call her Mum when he first moved in with her and thought of her as his second Mum.

'I've brought you a few more things love,' she replied showing him a brown case full of clothes. She fussed about for a minute or two unpacking the case and filling his kit bag and the small cabinet next to his bed with clothes.

'I had a visit from your teacher today, he told me your school friends are going home soon but he has been told that you're not fit to travel yet.'

'What's going to happen to me?' he asked.

'The plan is that you should stay here with Harry until you are both fit enough to go home and then the authorities will arrange your travel back to the Island.'

PC looked crestfallen and tears began to form in his eyes. 'But I want to go home with my friends,' he said quietly.

'I know love,' Glynis replied holding his hand. 'But the time will fly, and you don't want to go home with your leg in a cast now do you? It will be lovely to go back all fit and well so your real Mum will see you at your best.'

'You can also keep an eye on Harry here and make sure he's alright,' she added.

'How is Harry by the way,' she asked. 'He looks proper poorly.'

'He's OK Mum,' he replied. 'They are keeping him like that to make sure he doesn't move his head. They'll check him tomorrow and make sure he is OK.'

Glynis nodded in reply not as convinced as PC that Harry was alright. He certainly didn't look alright from where she was sitting.

She reached into her bag and pulled out a brown paper bag, 'I have brought you a treat,' she announced, placing the bag on PC's lap.

He looked inside and pulled out a freshly picked fig. 'Wow,' he exclaimed. 'My favourites! Can I have one now?'

'Of course, Peter love, they'll give you strength.'

PC wasn't sure why they would make him strong but tucked into the fig anyway. Glynis looked on happily. If PC had been watching her more carefully, he would have noticed a slight tear gathering in the corner of her eye. Glynis knew their time together was over. It had been agreed that the boys would stay together in the hospital and once they were both fit enough, they would go straight back to the Channel Islands. Her Peter, the son she had loved for the last 5 years, wasn't coming back to her home. He would be going back to his proper home and whatever was waiting for him there.

She had never been to the Channel Islands and until she met Peter had never even heard of Guernsey. At first she had felt a little awkward with a stranger in the house but the 9 year old, as he was then, was so polite and such a bundle of energy, that he was soon one of the family and willing to help whenever he could. In the first few months he had talked regularly of home and Glynis almost felt she knew Guernsey as well as a local. She knew he lived in St Peter Port at a place called Salerie Corner and that he loved to swim in the sea in the little harbour by his house. He was mad on football and dreamed of playing against Jersey in something called the Muratti. His Dad had played in a Muratti final and he wanted to emulate that achievement.

On an impulse she leaned forward, stroke his blond hair and kissed him on the forehead.

She couldn't help but wonder what would become of him and if he would achieve his dreams. She had grown to love this boy and she hoped he wouldn't forget her in the years to come. Soon she would need to say goodbye and who knows, it might be forever.

It was 8pm and she needed to get home.

'Right, I'm off,' she said in her gentle west country lilt.

'Night mum,' PC replied. 'Thanks for coming to see me.'

'You're welcome Peter, love.'

Glynis turned and headed for the door. As she left the ward, she turned and waved. PC waved back. As she walked down the corridor the tears began to flow.

PC picked up his Marvel Comic and started reading. He looked across at Harry who was still fast asleep.

I wish he would wake up, he thought.

At 10am it was time for lights out and one of the nurses came to check on them. She tucked PC in and checked Harry's vital signs.

'Goodnight PC,' she whispered. And pulled the curtains around their beds.

*****

The following morning after breakfast PC was helped out of bed and one of the nurses followed him to the bathroom so he could brush his teeth and go to the toilet.

Once he had finished his ablutions the nurses helped him get dressed, well at least on his top half, and then he started his exercises, walking up and down the ward to get used to his cast and crutches. The Doctor did his rounds mid-morning and checked on the boys. He spent some time with Harry checking his progress and he was happy enough with his progress to let him come around early and see how he felt. He was also pleased to see PC doing his exercises and making progress. Once he was done with the boys, he went off to check on the other patients in the ward.

PC had noticed as he walked up and down the ward that some of the soldiers were in quite a bad way. Many were heavily bandaged and several had broken limbs. Several of them had been brought back from prisoner of war camps in Germany and hadn't been that well treated so their injuries had got worse during the last few weeks of the war. The Doctors spent many hours with the soldiers helping them get back to full health, or at least well enough so that they can make the journey back to America.

As the morning wore on Harry came around from his long sleep and PC was there by his bed when he woke up.

'Hi Harry, welcome back, don't move,' were PC's first words to Harry.

Harry smiled at PC. 'Thank you.'

PC called the nurses over and they fussed around Harry making sure he was comfortable, giving him some water and sitting him up a little so he could have some lunch. PC sat in the chair next to Harry's bed and once the nurses were gone read him some of his comic while he fully recovered from his long sleep.

'How long have I been asleep?' he asked PC.

'A whole day,' PC replied. 'Wish I could sleep like that,' he joked.

Lunch arrived as they chatted about what had happened over the last 24 hours. They both tucked into sausages and mash, English style, one of the nurses helped Harry to cut up his sausages as his left wrist was still being supported in its cast. During lunch one of the nurses brought PC a book to read. It was one of the Hardy Boys Mystery stories called The Short-Wave Mystery.

That afternoon, after PC had done a few rounds of the ward on his crutches, PC sat down next to Harry and started reading the book out loud. As he did Harry shut his eyes and half asleep imagined himself tracking down the thieves like a true detective and solving the crime. The story took the Hardy Boys to Canada and Harry wondered what Canada and America were like. He promised himself that he would go there one day. While they had a cup of tea during the afternoon they spoke of America and asked one of the nurses what it was like.

She told the boys she came from a place called Chicago, known as the Windy City. She told them about tall buildings and huge railways. She had taken one of those trains to New York, another city full of tall buildings and from there had come to England on a freighter. Her trip had been just over a year ago and during the voyage one of the convoy of ships had been sunk by a German U-Boat and another had been damaged. She had been scared that their boat might be next. The tales thrilled the boys and filled their heads with thoughts of the war and the heroism of the sailors and all the people like the nurse who had made the journey to help keep Britain fighting in the war and ultimately triumph over Nazi Germany. As she was talking Sister Christine appeared and she shooed the nurse away to get on with some work.

'How are you boys doing?' She asked in her soft American accent.

'Fine Sister,' replied PC.

'What about you Harry?'

'I'm OK Sister,' Harry said quietly. 'Do you know how long I will be like this Sister?'

'It will be a while I'm afraid,' she answered smiling to try and reassure him. 'The Doctor will look at you again tomorrow and then we'll see what he suggests. Much will depend on the x-ray results and how badly you damaged your head when you hit the ground in the playground.

'You'll be fine Harry, just do what the Doctor tells you and you'll be back kicking a ball in no time.'

'Not sure if I want to kick a ball again,' Harry replied.

'Oh, you will,' Sister Christine replied knowingly. 'You like soccer, or football as you call it, too much to give up just yet. Once you are back home, you'll both be kicking the ball again before you know it.'

‘Even me with my broken leg?’ PC joined in.

‘Yes, even you,’ she replied with that lovely smile on her face.

‘Now chin up boys, tea will be here soon and who knows, you may get a visitor tonight.’

With that, Sister Christine went on to see some of the soldiers in the ward and they could hear her talking and laughing with some of them as she did her best to keep their spirits up too.

Both the boys thought that she was lovely.

They went back to their book but before PC could finish reading another chapter tea arrived and a meal of chicken, new potatoes and sweetcorn, covered in butter arrived for them to enjoy.

That evening Glynis came to see PC again and spent some of her time talking to Harry and reassuring him that she didn’t blame him for PC’s injuries. It was a Sunday and she told them the school had now broken up and the rumour was that a coach was going to take the Channel Island boys down to Weymouth next week so they could head home to the Channel Islands. Needless to say, there was no way that Harry and PC would be heading home any time soon and they needed to get used to that.

After chatting with them for an hour, Glynis left them, leaving some more figs. She told Harry she had a tree in her back garden and this year it had been very productive. She also brought them a few comics, several issues of the Beano and the Dandy to keep them occupied.

The boys chatted about the comics for a while after Glynis left, dividing them up so they both had something to read. A nurse came around at 10pm and drew the curtains around their beds and called for lights out. As they settled down, PC whispered across to Harry.

‘If the other Guernsey and Jersey kids go back next week, how are we going to get home?’

‘I don’t know,’ Harry replied. ‘I was thinking the same thing. I hope they don’t forget about us.’

Nothing else was said for a while as they both considered what might become of them and how they might make the journey home.

‘We’ll find a way,’ Harry suddenly said to PC, breaking the silence. ‘We’ll find a way.’

Sleep followed swiftly for both of them. Not doing much seemed to be as equally tiring as running around all day.

*****

Monday dawned bright and clear and the nurses woke the boys at 6am sharp. The routine was being ingrained in them now and they looked forward to the key moments of the day, usually associated with mealtimes. After breakfast a vicar, or Padre as the nurse called him, paid them a visit and sat chatting to them for a while. He asked where they were from and when they mentioned the Channel Islands he smiled and told them he had been to Jersey before the war and loved the place.

He also told them that he had heard that life in the Islands had been difficult over the last 12 months due to a lack of food and the essentials of life. That got the boys worried, but he went on to assure them that everyone had coped and red cross parcels had been sent to the Islands to help the Islanders survive the shortages. As far as he knew the Islands were trying to get back to normal now and had received a lot of support. He was sure they would find their families safe and well when they got home.

‘How are we going to get home?’ Harry asked the Padre.

‘I don’t know son,’ he replied with a gentle smile, ‘but I am sure they will send someone to come and get you or make the necessary arrangements to get you home. Just don’t worry about that, it isn’t your problem. Focus on getting better and let the powers that be worry about how to get you back to your families.’

The Padre noticed that Harry looked sad.

‘What’s the matter son?’ he asked with some concern.

‘I don’t have a family to go home to Padre. My mum died last year and my Dad was killed at Dunkirk.’

‘I’m sorry to hear that son, do you have some grandparents to go home to?’

‘Yes Padre, but they are old, and I don’t know if they’ll want to look after me.’

‘Listen Harry, I am sure they can’t wait for you to come home and certainly they will want you to live with them. You are the connection to their son and daughter-in-law, and they will want to meet you and talk about the last 5 years. Let’s face it, you’re not a baby anymore, so I am sure you won’t need much looking after. I’ll also give you a thought. Whatever happens, they are your link to the past. Talk to them, learn about their lives, because one day you may have children of your own and will want to pass on their story and your story to them.’

Harry smiled as did PC who had listened with interest. It was true, they had been away so long that everyone at home will want to hear what happened over the last 5 years, just as PC wanted to know what happened in Guernsey while the Germans were there. However, he still felt sorry for Harry, how horrible not to have a Mum and Dad waiting for him. The more he thought about it the more he couldn’t wait to see his real Mum and Dad again.

That determination manifested itself as soon as the Padre had walked off to visit some of the troops on the ward. PC quickly got himself dressed, leaving on his pyjama bottoms, then set off to the bathroom on his crutches, following up with some exercise, walking up and down the ward a few more times than he did the day before. One of the nurses kept an eye on him to make sure he was using the crutches correctly and smiled at the determined look on his face as the youngster battled to support his weight on his thin arms.

As he walked, he paid more attention to the other patients on the ward and a couple of them smiled at him as he walked past.

One of the men who was heavily bandaged around his body and had a sort of tent over his legs waved him over.

'Well howdy son,' he said in a strong southern drawl. 'What are you in here for?'

PC hopped over and stood next to the man's bed. 'I broke my leg playing football,' he said.

'Wow, I didn't think you Brits played football,' the American replied.

'We play football all the time,' PC replied not sure what the soldier meant.

'Oh, I guess you mean soccer,' the America said with a smile. 'That's like a kid's game.'

'No it's not,' PC replied somewhat indignantly. 'It's a man's game. My Dad played before the war. Anyway, what do you call football?'

'Football is what we Yanks play. It's a man's game, for real men. I used to be a running back before I joined up.'

If PC was meant to be impressed, he wasn't. He didn't have a clue what the soldier was talking about.

'If you want, I'll tell you all about Football while you here, if you are interested.'

'OK, I'm going to be here for a while,' PC said, trying to sound enthusiastic. 'I'll pop back this afternoon.'

'Great,' the America replied. 'Here, I've got something for you.'

The soldier reached into the cupboard next to his bed and brought out two small packets. He handed them over to PC who wondered what it was.

The American could see his confusion.

'It's chewing gum son. You chew it but don't swallow it. Give a packet to your pal.'

'Thanks,' PC said.

He smiled at the soldier and hobbled back to his bed. He was trying to work out why you would want to chew something but not swallow it. When he got back he gave a packet of the gum to Harry and told him he could chew it but he mustn't swallow it. They both unwrapped a stick of the gum and carefully pushed it in their mouths and started chewing. The taste was amazing and both the boys smiled and chewed happily, enjoying the new experience.

'When do we have to spit it out,' Harry asked. PC shrugged his shoulders and they sat there for a while happily chewing.

One of the nurses came passed and noticed them chewing.

'Where did you get that,' she asked sternly looking quite annoyed.

PC swallowed his gum; he was so shocked.

'One of the soldiers gave me it,' PC replied.

'Well we don't allow gum on the ward boys; people stick it to the beds and the tables. Spit it out.'

She held out her hand and Harry duly spat his gum into it.

'I've swallowed mine,' PC moaned. 'Am I going to die?'

The nurse got a tissue and wrapped it around Harry's gum.

'No, you're not going to die but don't let Sister catch you chewing gum. If she does, I can't vouch for what she might do.'

The boys both gulped and as soon as the nurse was gone, they hid the remaining gum at the back of their cupboards. Despite the warning they liked the taste so they would keep the gum for future use.

Before long lunch arrived. Today they had a small roast with beef and vegetables. Rice pudding followed and both lay back on their beds after their meals feeling extremely full and happy. Harry was happiest of all. Harry's mum had travelled from Jersey with him but after she died from TB, he had boarded at the school and the food there was nothing compared to what they were getting in the hospital. He also liked the attention of the nurses as by and large they had been left to their own devices in the school.

Both boys dozed for some of the afternoon then PC got out of bed again and did some more exercise, getting a thumbs up from a couple of the soldiers. In the other bed. Harry wished he could join in but as he wasn't allowed up, he read a little from one of the comics, struggling to keep his eyes open. Later in the afternoon the Doctor came to see Harry and told him that he had indeed fractured his skull but there seemed to be little evidence of internal damage to his brain, which was good. To be safe he wanted to keep him in bed for at least a week, maybe two, until he was sure the bone was healing correctly, and the headaches had completely gone away. He told Harry that as he was still young the bone should heal much quicker than with older patients so his recovery should be complete in a month or 6 weeks.

He then went to see PC and asked him how the exercises were going and if he had any pain. Once he was happy all was well, he suggested his healing time would be around 6 weeks and as the schools were going next week the two boys would be kept together here until they were both fit to travel.

The news was disappointing for both boys, but they drew comfort that they would not be on their own. Their friendship over the last couple of days had started to grow and both were happy that they would be together. Worse things happen as Harry's Dad used to say.

Tea came along, this time it was a light sandwich and some fruit.

Glynis visited PC again that evening and one of the teachers from the school came to see Harry. He confirmed that the Channel Island boys and girls would be heading home on Wednesday. Both boys looked shocked though they had known the others would be going home soon, having the day mentioned seemed to make it more real.

'What will happen to us?' PC butted in. 'When are we going home?'

Mr. Bateman, the teacher, didn't know but said as soon as they got back to the Islands, they would make the necessary arrangements to get the boys back home as soon as they were fit enough to travel. They chatted about the journey home and he explained that a bus would be taking them all to Weymouth to get a ferry back to the Islands.

Before long the nurses were chasing the visitors out and Glynis and Mr. Bateman made their way home. The boys looked at each other.

'I wish we were going home on Wednesday,' PC said looking at Harry.

'Let's make a pact,' Harry replied. 'As soon as we are fit enough, we'll get out of here and go home.'

PC eased himself out of bed and hopped across to Harry. He stuck out his hand and Harry shook it.

'Deal,' PC said. They shook hands again and they both smiled.

Lights out came at 10pm as always, and they both fell asleep quickly.

On Wednesday the day fell into the normal rhythm until just before lunch when a bunch of boys from Taunton School came on to the ward with Mr. Bateman to say goodbye. The ward buzzed with noise for a while and Sister Christine tutted at the noise and tried to keep everyone under control so as not to annoy the other patients in the ward. The friends signed their casts and after half an hour they all left, and the ward returned to relative peace and quiet for lunch.

PC did some more exercises in the afternoon and before long tea was being delivered at 6pm on the dot.

That evening Glynis came to visit at 7pm but she had some bad news for PC.

'Peter Love, we are going to see my Mum in Yorkshire for a while.'

‘Oh, when are you coming back?’

‘I’m not sure love,’ she replied. ‘We might be gone for a while though. In fact, there’s a chance you will be back home in Guernsey by the time we get back.’

PC looked at Glynis and his eyes started to fill with tears at the reality of what was happening. She leaned across and gave PC a huge hug as he sobbed on her shoulder.

‘It doesn’t mean we won’t see each other again. Maybe we can come and visit you in Guernsey and you know you will always have a place to stay if you want to come here.’

‘When are you going?’ PC asked quietly.

‘Tomorrow morning,’ she whispered.

‘What!’ PC exclaimed.

‘Sorry love, I wanted to tell you before but didn’t want you to worry. I had always planned to go as soon as you went back to Guernsey, but as you are not coming home, I decided to go as soon as I could. Mum isn’t very well and needs looking after and there’s only me who can do that.’

PC knew Glynis had a Mum up north and she was quite old. He had seen pictures of her and knew that they exchanged letters often but he didn’t know she was ill.

Glynis kissed PC on the forehead.

‘You’re a wonderful lad and I have enjoyed every minute of you being with me. Your parents should be very proud of you. Give them my love and tell them I hope to meet them one day soon.’

With that she got up and walked to the door. Before she left the ward, she turned to look at PC one last time and waved. He could see the tears running down her face. She mouthed 'Love you' and went through the door.

PC was inconsolable and one of the nurses came to sit with him for a while. Harry wished he could do something to help but he couldn't think of anything useful to say.

Before lights out, and after he had quietened down, PC lay there staring out of the window.

'Are you OK? Harry asked, breaking the silence.

'Yeah,' PC lied.

'If I could move, I would come over and give you a hug,' Harry said quietly.

'Thanks.' PC replied.

'Remember our pact mate.' Harry said looking across at PC. 'Friends forever?'

'Friends forever,' PC replied.

As the lights went out both boys lay awake for some time trying to think what would happen to them now they were on their own.

Both eventually fell into a fitful sleep.

*****

Thursday morning dawned bright and clear. Breakfast consisted of something called Grits along with bacon and scrambled eggs. The boys had never heard of Grits, but they quite liked it. This American food was starting to grow on them. They were a bit quiet knowing all their friends and PC's adopted family were now all gone. The nurses caught the mood and made a fuss of them, even Sister Christine spent a little more time with the boys. PC did a few more exercises and even got to walk to the front door to get a bit of fresh air. Everyone tried to be very positive with the boys and even a few of the soldiers smiled and gave PC the thumbs up as he walked past.

After lunch the Doctor came to see how the boys were progressing and it was agreed that they both needed fresh air. He suggested to Sister Christine that Harry be given regular outings in the gardens of the Hospital in a wheelchair, with his head held secure in a brace. He prescribed a daily constitutional, when the weather was good and if possible, they should start tomorrow.

The news brought a smile to their faces. It felt as if they were making progress.

As he turned to leave, he said to the boys. 'Remember, every day you are here is a day nearer to you going home. Keep positive and you'll be home before you know it.'

That evening after tea the boys chatted about going out. PC had an extra walk up and down the corridor and spent ten minutes talking to one of the GI's as the nurses referred to them.

Steve told him tales of the war and how he had been wounded and captured in the Bastogne on Christmas day in 1944 during the Battle of the Bulge as it was known. The weather had been horrendous, and he had lain injured for two days before being found by German troops and taken prisoner. This had resulted in frostbite on his injured leg and the last few months had seen a lot of deterioration in his condition until he had been released by the retreating Germans in April 1945. He had returned to England after a short stay in a field hospital in France.

The Doctors there had removed the lower half of his left leg and the toes from his right foot. Since being admitted to the hospital in Taunton, he had undergone several operations to ensure the remains of his left leg could support a prosthetic so he would be able to learn to walk again. He was also in poor physical shape when he had been found, suffering from pneumonia and some skin issues. The doctors were helping him regain his strength so he could cope with the stresses of using the crutches that were waiting for him. Steve also told PC that if it hadn't been for the friendship of fellow GI's, who had helped him move around, he reckoned the Germans would have shot him to get him out of the way months ago.

PC was amazed at the story and promptly retold the tale to Harry who was equally amazed. He wished he could go and talk to the GI's too. PC also came back with some more gum so the boys enjoyed a crafty chew while the nurses were busy doing their evening round as they resumed their reading. New Marvel comics seemed to appear every day and kept them enthralled with tales of Captain America, the Human Torch and many other comic book heroes.

What the boys were also realising was that they were surrounded by heroes of a different sort as they learned more about the men they shared the ward with, and the hardships they had been through. They were so relieved that it was all over and hopefully men like these would never have to go to war again.

The next day the boys were eager to get outside and enjoy the sunshine which was streaming through the windows. They had to go through their normal morning routine first and PC took more turns up and down the ward in preparation for their adventure. The boys were dressed, and Harry was transferred to a wheelchair by the nurses. They took a lot of time making sure he was moved carefully, not to disturb his neck brace, and to see that he was comfortable. They left him in the chair for lunch and a special table was placed in front of him so he could eat.

As soon as lunch was over the anticipation began to build as Sister Christine appeared to oversee the operation and to ensure everything happened efficiently, in true army fashion.

It was made clear to the nurses that boys were not to go far and they should not be out for longer than an hour. One of the nurses was put in charge and told to stay with them for the duration of the expedition.

As soon as all was in place, the doors to the ward were wedged open and with Sister Christine in the lead, the procession made its way out into the garden. Outside the ward there was a short corridor which led to an outside door and freedom as PC called it. Harry being pushed by their allotted nurse followed Sister Christine with PC on his crutches walking behind and another nurse following behind to close the doors and keep an eye on him.

Once in the garden they walked along a path to where a wooden bench was located in the sunshine, surrounded by beautiful flower gardens and facing a small fountain. Butterflies, bees and birds were everywhere. Harry's wheelchair was parked next to the bench and his nurse sat next to him, leaving enough room for PC to sit if he wanted. Sister Christine tucked a blanket she had been carrying around Harry's legs and urged PC not to overdo it as he took to walking across the lawn to the fountain and watching the goldfish swimming around under the waterlilies.

PC walked back to Harry.

'I wish we could kick a ball about, don't you?' he suggested to Harry

'Too right,' Harry replied. 'Can't wait to get my boots on again.'

The nurse smiled. 'You boys will have to wait a while before you are running around again,' she told them. 'Will you play together?' She added.

'Certainly not,' Harry replied quickly.

‘We’ll always be on different sides, miss,’ PC added. ‘Different Islands you see.’

‘That’s a shame,’ the nurse replied with a smile.

‘Where are you from miss?’ PC asked.

‘A little town called Fargo in North Dakota,’ she replied a little wistfully. ‘I can’t wait to get home and see my folks,’ she added.

‘What’s it like?’ Harry asked.

The nurse tapped the seat next to her in a signal to PC to sit down.

Once he was sitting, she began to tell the boys all about Fargo and North Dakota. They learned that Fargo was established on the Red River in the 1870’s and had been named after one of the founders of the Wells Fargo company that used to run stagecoaches across America. It was on the territory of the Sioux Indians and was a sleepy sort of town surrounded by plains with not a hill in sight in any direction. She lived in an old wooden building which had survived the great fire of 1893. Her family history included cowboys who had hunted buffalo and further back, men who had fought in the Union Army during the American Civil War.

The boys were enthralled and asked if she knew Annie Oakley and Wild Bill Hickok who they had read about in comics but she told them they were a bit before her time though her father had seen Annie Oakley perform in Buffalo Bill’s Wild West show once many years ago.

‘Wow,’ said PC. ‘I always wanted to be a cowboy and ride the range like the Lone Ranger.’

‘Well if you ever come to Fargo, I’ll see what I can do,’ she told the boys, beaming away at them, pleased that she had fired their imagination.

‘My name’s Catherine by the way.’

She looked at her watch.

‘Not long to go now,’ she told them. ‘Do you fancy a turn around the garden?’

‘Yes please,’ they replied in unison.

She got up and turned Harry’s wheelchair back to the path and with PC walking alongside, they took a 15-minute walk around the grounds.

Sister Christine was waiting for them looking at her watch as they arrived back at the door.

‘Good timing boys,’ she said smiling at the nurse and holding the door open for them.

Once back inside the nurses helped Harry back into bed and PC was told to rest before doing anything else.

Suffice to say all they could talk about was Cowboys and Indians as the afternoon swiftly passed into early evening when tea arrived.

After tea the Doctor came to visit and he was pleased to see them so relaxed and looking well, all things considered. He was convinced the outing had done them good. He was happy the excursions should continue but felt an hour a day was enough for the time being.

That evening the book and comics came out again until one of the nurses brought them some books of plain paper and colouring pencils. They ended up drawing Cowboys and

Indians, as well as they could, and vowed to show Nurse Catherine their work the following day.

*****

The next day flew past until it was time for their next outing. Nurse Catherine was there again, and she had brought them a surprise. She had two books for them to read. One was the Lone Ranger Rides Again and the other was called the American Cowboy. Both boys were so pleased they couldn't say thanks enough times.

They were looking forward to their outing but equally couldn't wait to get back now and start reading their new books.

This time they went a bit further until they arrived in a car park which was full of military vehicles of different types. Ambulances and jeeps were in the majority and the boys were fascinated to see uniformed soldiers coming and going in the jeeps, some of the iconic vehicles still sporting machine guns and rifles.

'I'd love a trip in one of those,' PC whispered to Harry.

Catherine heard the comment.

'Maybe when Harry can take off the neck brace, we can arrange a drive out,' Catherine suggested. 'I know a couple of the officers who might be happy to take you out for a ride.'

'That would be great miss,' PC replied.

They headed back to the ward where Sister Christine was waiting for them again. All the time the depression they had experienced from been left behind was being turned into excitement for the future thanks to the anticipation of better things to come. Sister Christine knew what was happening and smiled at their eager faces and the excitement in their voices.

Time was no longer dragging for the boys and she could see them growing in confidence as each day passed.

And so, a routine began. Each morning PC would exercise indoors, and, in the afternoon, they would journey outside, and he would walk the grounds while Harry would be pushed around in his wheelchair. When he wasn't exercising, PC would talk to the other patients in the ward, hearing tales of the heroism, pain and sadness they had experienced during the Second World War. He learned of places he had never heard of before and of battles that had changed the lives of countless people and ended the lives of countless more.

Each day he would pass on those tales to Harry and together they would talk about everything from the war to cowboys and from time to time football.

After a couple of weeks of this routine the Doctor came to visit and decided it was time to take off Harry's neck brace. Harry's smile seemed to spread from ear to ear as Nurse Catherine and the Doctor undid the brace. Harry rubbed his neck in relief and gingerly turned his head from side to side.

'How does it feel?' The Doctor asked.

'Feels a bit stiff.' Harry replied.

'You'll be fine,' the Doctor advised. 'Just don't try and do too much too soon. No heading that football just yet.'

He laughed, pointing at PC's leather football sitting on the windowsill.

'I won't,' Harry smiled back.

'Keep an eye on him,' the Doctor said to Nurse Catherine with a wink as he left, giving the boys a quick wave before he disappeared through the door.

The next day there was an excitement on the ward and the boys, curious as to what was going on, asked Sister Christine as she was passing, what was happening.

'The boys fighting the Japanese have just dropped something called an atomic bomb on a city called Hiroshima. They reckon it will bring an end to the war. Apparently, they have given the Japanese the chance to surrender so the war could be over real soon.' She gave them a thumbs up and a big smile then went off to calm everyone down.

They could hear her shouting at the other nurses to stop celebrating and to get all the patients back in their beds. It sounded to the boys as if she was having a hard time getting everyone to settle down.

PC turned to Harry. 'What's an atomic bomb?'

'No idea.' Harry replied. 'But it sounds… big!'

They both laughed, totally oblivious to what the bomb meant or what it had done. Their routine continued then three days later news came that a second bomb had been dropped on another Japanese city. This time it was somewhere called Nagasaki. Five days later, on the 15th August, the real party started when news of the unconditional surrender of Japan was announced. The second world war was finally over.

The smiles on the ward were huge and balloons and ribbons were produced as if by magic. Even Sister Christine joined in with the party spirit and magically some champagne had been found and was being drunk on the ward. It was like the best Christmas party anyone could ever remember. The boys were allowed a small sip of champagne, but neither of them liked it and both wondered what all the fuss was about. They were allowed a Coca Cola instead.

The next morning Harry had the cast removed from his wrist which came as a great relief and PC was told his cast would come off next week.

Both boys could now walk without too much help, though PC still had to use crutches, but he was now allowed to put some weight on his broken leg. He had even been allowed to use a stick when he went outside the ward on occasion but winced occasionally if he put too much weight on his bad leg. Harry seemed the better of the two but was still not allowed to move too quickly and when he went out in the jeeps, he had to put the neck brace back on.

After Harry had his cast removed the Doctor came to visit and told the boys he would be assessing their situation soon. The chances were, now that the war was over on both fronts, that the patients and the hospital staff will soon be heading back to America and there would be no place for the boys here. He would need to decide when they would be able to go back home. Much would depend on whether or not they could travel safely and what arrangements could be made to get them passage back to the Islands. If not, then he suggested they might be moved to another hospital. He promised to let them know as soon as possible and with his big Hollywood smile and a wink, he left them to their usual exercise routine.

PC and Harry looked at each other.

'I wonder when we'll get to go home?' PC whispered to Harry.

'I wish I was going to America with Nurse Catherine and Sister Christine.' Harry whispered back. 'I've got nothing to go back to in Jersey, just my old Granddad and Grandma. I can't even remember what they look like.'

He ran his hands through his thick black hair which he was starting to style like some of the troops on the ward. He would like to have been an American.

‘I want to go home Harry.’ PC blurted out. ‘I want to see Guernsey again and see my parents again. Maybe you can come and live with me. We can go and visit America together when we are a bit older.’

Harry thought for a moment.

‘That’s a nice idea.’ Harry said quietly. ‘We need to stick together though.’ PC nodded in response.

‘Let’s see what the Doc comes up with and then we’ll decide what to do.’ Harry continued. ‘Thank you for your kind offer PC, but I guess I need to go back to Jersey if I can and see what has happened to my grandparents and tell them what happened over here. But we’ll make that journey together whatever happens.’

He held out his hand with a determined look on his face. PC reached out from his perch on the edge of his bed and shook Harry’s hand.

‘That’s a promise Harry. That’s a promise.

Chapter Two

Another couple of weeks passed, during which time PC had his cast removed. He felt so much better for being free of the cast and immediately tested his leg, somewhat gingerly, with a quick walk around the garden, using just his stick for support. He found he could walk unaided quite well so in the next few days, crutches and sticks became a thing of the past.

On a few occasions Sister Christine allowed them out in a jeep. The boys were so excited and happily took their place on the narrow back seat and imagined they were able to man the machine gun which was still fixed to the jeep. One of the nurses would take the passenger seat and a GI would drive them around Taunton and occasionally into the surrounding countryside. The driver explained that they were in a Willys MB jeep that had seen service in France and Germany. It had been returned to England in May after the war in Europe was over.

On one occasion they went as far as a place called Bridgewater and from there to the mouth of the river Parrett where they had a glimpse of the sea. That made them wistful for the Islands, where the sea had been a part of their daily lives.

They really enjoyed their trips although they were often far too short, in their opinion, as they wanted to explore more of the countryside around Taunton.

The boys tried to imagine where the jeep had been and imagined it crossing into Germany with General Omar Bradley sitting where they were sitting, leading the charge to reach Berlin and finish the war.

On the 28th August, the Doctor surprised the boys by visiting them early in the morning, instead of during his usual evening rounds.

He sat down on the edge of Harry's bed first and spoke to him directly.

'Harry, I am happy for you to go home straight away. I have been speaking to the authorities in Jersey and they will provide you with safe passage from Weymouth to Jersey in a weeks' time. You are going to stay with us for 5 more days and then a jeep will drive you down to Weymouth where you will stay for the night before catching the boat home.'

'What's going to happen to PC sir,' he asked.

'I'm coming to him,' the Doctor replied, with a smile.

He turned to PC.

'Peter, you are not quite ready to go home. I would like to see that limp disappear before we let you go but time is against us. Today is Tuesday and we have arranged that on Sunday you will be transferred to another hospital, probably in Southampton but we are still making the final arrangements, and then after some more physiotherapy and rehabilitation you will be sent back to Guernsey. I have spoken to the authorities there and though things are still a bit chaotic they will make the arrangements to get you on a boat once you are given the all clear to travel.

'But I want to stay with Harry, Sir.'

'Sorry son, that just won't be possible, you need to go your separate ways.'

The boys both looked down, deep in thought. The Doctor saw they were upset and softened his voice.

'I'm sorry boys, we are starting to pack up and ship home. You need to do the same. The war is over now for all of us and we must get back to our homes and try and restart our lives and get back to normal. You have your whole lives ahead of you and you'll have plenty of chances to meet up again.' He smiled but both boys kept silent.

'You've become great friends here in Taunton, being apart for a few weeks, months or even years won't change that. Just keep in touch with each other and before you know it you'll meet up again and be able to talk about these experiences and who knows, maybe you'll come to visit America one day and we can have a beer somewhere and I can show you around my home town.'

Harry looked up.

'Where do you live, sir?' Harry asked.

'I live in a place called Boston, Massachusetts, son, and you are welcome in my house any time. I'll give you a card with my address on it so if you do ever come to America you can look me up. I can show you where the Boston Tea Party happened which started the War of Independence and got us away from you Brits.' He laughed. 'I'll bring you my card after supper tonight when I do my rounds.'

'Thank you, sir.' Harry said as the Doctor got up from his bedside.

The Doctor smiled and winked. 'Thank you for being great patients' boys. Glad we could help you get better.'

'Thank you,' the boys replied in unison half smiling as he went through the door and out of the ward.

They sat for a moment in silence then Harry went across to sit next to PC so they could talk quietly.

'I'm not leaving here without you PC. If we are going home, we are going home together.'

PC smiled. 'I don't want to hold you back Harry. If you can get back home just go, I'll be alright.'

'That's not what we agreed.' Harry replied. 'We shook on it remember, and a promise is a promise.'

Harry thought for a moment. 'We have 5 days to come up with a plan. We need to watch their routines and work out how to get out of here - we may need some help.'

They spent the next ten minutes before breakfast trying to come up with a plan to get out of Taunton. After that the days routine began in earnest, with PC heavily motivated to work as hard as he could to make sure he would be fit enough for the journey ahead.

During the next three days the boys spent some time getting their kit-bags packed ready to leave the hospital. No-one questioned what they were doing as they were due to leave anyway. PC spoke to Steve, one of the GI's on the ward he had befriended, who, after a little persuading agreed to help as best, he could, even though he was largely confined to bed. Steve even gave him some English money as he said he was due to be shipped back to America soon and would have no need of the £5 note and assorted coins he gave him.

The boys also collected the names and addresses of the Doctor, Steve, Sister Christine and Nurse Catherine as well as a few more of the GI's and they promised to write to them and let them know how they got on when they got back to their respective islands and maybe visit, if they ever travelled to America. The addresses were from across the United States, but the boys didn't really appreciate just how big America was. No-one was seeking to upset them, particularly at this time, so everyone said how they would be welcome in their homes whenever they chose to visit and all wanted postcards from the Islands so they could see what they were like.

On Saturday night they were ready to implement their plan. They had squirreled away some food, including fruit and meat from their meals and their bags were packed. They had noted that the doors to the ward were locked at midnight, so they knew they had to get away before then. That night after the final round and the Doctor had said his final goodbye, they went to bed fully dressed, hiding their pyjamas under their pillows and drawing their bedclothes up to their chins. Everything they wanted to take with them, apart from their books, were in their bags.

At 11.30, Steve started to groan and the nurse who was on night duty walked across to see if he was alright. Steve complained about a pain in his leg and the nurse drew the curtain around his bed so she could have a look and see what was wrong. As soon as the curtain closed the boys slipped out of bed, packed their beds to make it look as if they were still under the covers, stuffed their books into their bags and headed for the door. They were almost there when PC stopped.

'My ball,' he whispered to Harry.

Without waiting for a reply, he tip toed back to his bed and took his beloved ball down from the windowsill where it had been since they arrived in the hospital.

Harry was at the door waiting for him and pushed it open to let him pass before following PC down the corridor. From there they slipped out into the garden and crept away towards the hospital gates.

Back in the ward Steve had calmed down and the nurse had given him some aspirin and resumed her seat at the top of the ward. At midnight she did a quick check of all the beds and locked the doors to the ward and settled down for her night shift with a magazine and a cup of coffee. She didn't notice the missing ball or the missing boys.

Outside it was chilly but not cold and the boys made their way towards the gate and the guard house.

Being a military hospital, a guard house had been placed at the gates and the troops stationed there had made sure everyone coming and going were "authorised" to be visiting the hospital. However, since the end of the war they had not been as strict as they might have been and tonight, the two GI's with Military Police badges on their sleeves, were in the guard house playing cards to while away the time. A wooden barrier was all that stood between the boys and the open road. The trouble was that piece of roadway was bathed in the light from the Guard House.

The two paused as they assessed the situation and then Harry pulled PC back a bit so they could talk.

'We're going to have to be very quiet and slip under the barrier.' Harry said. 'It would be best if we kept close to the Guard House, keeping below the windows.'

'OK,' said PC. 'I'll go first.'

Before Harry could reply, PC crept forward towards the Guard House and knelt down under the window ledge. He looked back and got a thumbs up from Harry who was watching the guards. PC turned and started to creep past the door just as one of the Guards got up and walked towards the door. Harry froze in horror as the two of them looked as if they would literally bump into other.

Totally unaware of the soldier's movements, PC kept going and as he approached the door he scrambled as fast as he could through the edge of the pool of light which emanated from the Guard House windows. The guard grabbed the door handle just as PC was passing but paused to say something to his fellow GI before laughing and opening the door. PC could hear the other guard say - 'You calling me a cheat?' and laughing in a good humoured way as he stepped outside.

PC just managed to slip around the back of the Guard House as the GI took a few steps into the centre of the driveway, and then after pausing to look around, he walked across the drive and into the garden. Both boys could hear the GI having a pee and the sound of a zipper before he walked back across the drive, took one last look around and then stepped back into the Guard House. 'Fancy a coffee Joe?' were the last words the boys heard before the door shut.

Both boys' hearts were thumping out of their chests as they waited a full five minutes before moving. PC was first to creep back around to the front of the Guard House and wave Harry forward. Harry crept across and followed the same path as PC, this time without incident and soon the two friends were reunited on the outside of the Hospital grounds.

A pale moon hung over them as they stood by the side of the road. PC wore his faithful Guernsey over a grey shirt and a pair of dark grey school shorts with long blue football socks and his battered black school shoes. He had his kitbag slung over his back and his football under his right arm. Harry had a black V neck jumper over a tattered white shirt, long grey trousers and black socks with his old black school shoes. He too had a kitbag slung over his shoulder. He wore his school cap over his jet black hair.

'Which way?' PC whispered.

'South.' Harry replied.

'Which way is that? PC replied.

'I was hoping you knew' Harry answered with a big smile. They laughed and both agreed they should go right.

With that they headed off into the night, taking their first steps on their long journey home.

They followed a road, which they had travelled on before in one of their jeep expeditions, until they saw the lights of a vehicle heading in their direction. They skipped off the road into some trees and made their way down a slope until they found a stream. Both boys took a nervous drink from the fresh water using their cupped hands. In the light of the moon they saw a path along the edge of the stream and decided to follow it and see where it came out. They didn't know it but they were following the Galmington Stream which would take them into the centre of Taunton.

After an eventful walk along the stream, which included a few slips and slides and a wet foot for Harry, they came across a main road. They decided to head to the right as they could see some buildings up ahead and were soon walking into the heart of Taunton. They kept quiet and tried to keep in the shadows though there didn't seem to be a soul in sight. As they rounded a corner into Corporation Street, PC spotted a policeman making his way towards them on the opposite side of the road. They dodged into an alley and waited behind some dustbins until he had walked past. After they had waited a few minutes they ventured back to the road to check if it was all clear. PC had a good look around then ushered Harry out and they continued their journey on to East Street before they came across a road sign. This told them if they turned right, they would be heading to Chard, Honiton, Lyme Regis and Sidmouth.

'Lyme Regis is on the south coast,' PC whispered to Harry. 'It's where they go to find dinosaurs. I read it in a magazine.'

'OK.' Harry replied quietly. 'Let's follow the road to Lyme Regis and find a dinosaur.'

They both grinned at each other and after checking the road was clear, they headed down Silver Street on to the South Road and the road to Chard.

Thankful for the moon they walked for another hour, passing the gates of Kings College and Richard Huish College on the way.

They were soon out in the countryside and as they were both getting tired decided to take a rest in a barn they had spotted alongside the road. The clouds seemed to be building so they felt it was safer to stop walking while they could still see. Sneaking inside the small door at the side of the main barn door, they could see by the streams of moonlight coming in through gaps in the wooden walls that it was full of bales of hay stacked to the ceiling. They found a ledge amongst the bales and settled down for what was left of the night. They were soon sound asleep.

Chapter Three

The boys woke to the sound of a tractor and the rattling of the main barn door.

Chains were being unlocked and the main doors were being swung open revealing a trailer full of hay sitting behind a red tractor. They sat blinking and rubbing their eyes in the bright light and were soon spotted by the farmer as he came around from the side of the barn after securing the doors open.

'What have we yer?' He asked talking to no-one in particular.

He walked over to the boys and stood with his hands on his hips staring at them for a few moments. The boys were paralyzed with fear not knowing what he would do next.

He was wearing a set of dark blue overall, wellington boots and flat cap and smoked a large pipe.

'Guess you boys must be hungry?' He said, his ruddy face bursting into a big smile.

Harry and PC looked at each other.

'Yes sir,' they said in unison.

'Come on then,' the Farmer said, 'help me unload this lot and I'll treat you to some breakfast.'

'Thank you, sir.' Harry said as the boys climbed down off the bales.

'Less of the sir please boys,' the farmer replied. 'My name is William, but my friends call me Bill. Help me with this lot and you can call me Bill.'

'Thank you, sir, I mean Bill,' said PC. 'My name is Peter, but my friends call me PC, and this is my best friend Harry.'

Bill shook hands with the boys in turn and they went to work.

Bill reversed the trailer into the barn and then they attacked the pile of bales. Bill had a long fork and effortlessly threw the bales on to the top of the pile. PC had clambered to the top and made sure the bales were lined up properly while Harry dragged the bales on the trailer to Bill, so he didn't have to move as he threw the bales up to PC.

Soon, they were all sweating as the pile of bales on the trailer rapidly shrank and the stack in the barn got bigger and bigger.

After an hour of hard work, the trailer was empty, and Bill announced that it was, 'time for breakfast,' and added 'well done lads.' The boys, smiling, got their kit and sat on the back of the trailer as Bill drove to his farmhouse.

PC sat hugging his precious ball as they drove across several fields and down narrow tracks leaving a trail of windblown hay behind them. Soon they were approaching an idyllic farmhouse with an inviting trail of white smoke coming from one of its chimney pots. Chickens were picking at whatever they could find in the front yard and a black and white dog sat on the step of a small porch waiting eagerly for his master to return. Down each side of the house were vegetable patches and fruit trees, many laden with apples. A washing line was in full use in the early morning sun and amongst the vegetable patches a scarecrow, wearing old blue overalls and wellington boots, stood guard over the fruits of the farmers labour.

Even before the tractor and trailer stopped, the smell of bacon had reached their nostrils and the boys were almost drooling as the lovely smell made them realise just how hungry they were.

Bill jumped down from the tractor and invited the boys into the house.

‘Let me introduce you to my wife,’ he said, a hint of pride in his voice.

He opened the front door. ‘Jean, come and see what I found,’ he shouted into the house.

‘Wipe your shoes boys,’ he asked, then waved them in.

Before they could get in the front door a short, buxom woman appeared in the door. After a moment of surprise at seeing the boys she burst into a beautiful smile.

‘I was expecting a dead fox,’ she announced in her west country accent. ‘He’s always bringing them home to show me, like I’m interested in a dead fox.’

She laughed and the boys couldn’t help but laugh too as the sound was so infectious.

‘This is PC, and this is Harry.’ Bill explained pointing to the boys. ‘They have just helped me unload the trailer and I have promised them breakfast in return.’

‘Did you now?’ Jean replied. ‘Well my name is Jean and it looks like I need to put more eggs and bacon on the aga. Come in and welcome to Fosgrove Farm.’

The boys followed Jean into the farmhouse and straight into the kitchen which overlooked the back garden and a field full of sheep.

‘If you need the loo boys, it’s out the back door at the end of the path. Wash your hands before you sit down.’

The boys dutifully washed their hands in the big sink and then sat down at the kitchen table while Jean worked away at getting their breakfast ready.

Soon they were tucking into bacon and eggs with chunks of bread and a steaming cup of tea.

The dog, which they found out was called Laddie, sat staring up at Bill as they ate their breakfast and was rewarded with a piece of bacon. That resulted in Jean giving Bill one of her stares - they both laughed. They certainly seemed a very happy couple.

All was going well until Bill asked the question Jean was probably dying to ask.

'So, what were you doing sleeping in our barn then boys?'

Harry looked at PC and both were unsure what to say.

'Are you on the run from the police?' Jean asked seriously.

'No.' PC replied, not sure what else to say.

He had always been taught that honesty was the best policy so after an uncomfortable minute's silence he told them the whole story.

'We are both from the Channel Islands and were sent here while the Germans were occupying the Islands. We were due to go back to the Islands a few weeks ago but got injured in a playground football accident and have been in hospital until yesterday. They told us we had to go home separately but we want to go home together so we decided to leave the hospital and make our own way home. We sneaked away in the night and got as far as your barn before we needed some sleep. Sorry.'

'Well,' said Jean. 'We should be sorry. Bill shouldn't have got you working if you are just out of hospital.'

She smiled at them. 'Well you're safe here and you are going in the right direction.'

She thought for a moment. ‘Why don’t you both stay here for a couple of nights and let the dust settle, then once you have had a bit more rest you can restart your journey?’

Bill smiled at his wife.

‘What a good idea Jean. What do you think boys?’

He saw them hesitate for a moment. ‘There’s lamb and roast potatoes for tea.’

That swung it and both boys nodded smiling.

‘That’s settled then.’ Jean said. ‘I’ll go and make up the spare room. We have twin beds in there in case any of my family come to stay.’

She got up and disappeared upstairs.

‘Fancy a tour of the farm.’ Bill offered.

‘Yes please,’ the boys replied.

‘Come on then.’ Bill said standing up from the table.

He walked to the bottom of the stairs and shouted up to Jean.

‘Taking the boys out for a tour of the farm. Will be back by noon Luv.’

‘Okay Billy Boy, have fun.’ Jean shouted back, accompanied by the sound of sheets being shook out over the beds.

With that the three of them headed out to the tractor. Bill disconnected the trailer then drove across to a large shed where he brought out a smaller box style trailer. He hooked it up to the tractor and put a bale of hay in the trailer for the boys to sit on.

They climbed into the back and Bill drove them out into the fields, explaining as they went about the farm and how they specialised in sheep farming, but how they also had some cattle for milk in one of the far fields. On the tour they saw a pond with ducks, the farmers small herd of black and white cows and lots and lots of sheep.

When they got back to the house, he introduced them to the chickens and found Jean in the vegetable patch digging potatoes ready for tea.

After Jean had shown them their room, they sat down for a ploughman's lunch before Bill suggested they have a rest during the afternoon while he went out to carry on stacking hay in the barn.

Jean went back out into the garden and started weeding their vegetable patch.

PC popped upstairs and got his football and they went out into the field behind the house for a gentle kick around, followed by a curious Laddie. The dog laid down watching every roll of the ball as the friends kicked the ball back and forwards to each other.

After a few minutes Harry asked PC how his leg was feeling.

'Not too bad,' he replied. 'Wouldn't want to run too far on it but it seems to be much better. How's your head?'

'Haven't noticed it thankfully but I'll not head a ball for a little while yet.'

They wandered off to one of the stone walls surrounding the field and sat with their backs to the wall, enjoying the feel of the afternoon sun on their faces. They made sure they found a patch clear of sheep droppings, but bits of wool seemed to be everywhere around them.

‘Are you happy staying here for a night or two?’ PC asked Harry.

‘I think so but let’s not get too comfortable eh!’ Harry replied. ‘Let’s not forget our mission.’

PC laughed. ‘I’ll not forget. Come on, let’s see if we can help Jean with the weeding.’

The boys ran off to see Jean and soon they were collecting apples and picking loganberries ready for her to make a crumble for them to eat tomorrow.

By the time Bill returned tea was ready to eat and the apples were chopped and soaking in a bowl with the loganberries.

After a hearty tea Jean got out an old battered box of Ludo and they played a few games before Jean declared it was bedtime.

They all paid a visit to the loo down the garden path and then washed their hands and faces in the sink before bedtime. Jean warned them that the couple would be up with the lark next morning but told them to rest and not get up too early. The small clock in their bedroom said 9.30 as the candles were blown out and the boys fell into a deep sleep. All the fresh air had made them extremely tired.

Bill starting out at 6am to work on the farm didn’t wake the boys but the smell of more bacon frying did the trick and they came down stairs just in time to see Bill come back in after a couple of hours work and join them for another breakfast of bacon and eggs.

‘Anything you want to do today boys?’

‘Can we feed the ducks?’ PC randomly blurted out.

Jean laughed. 'I think we can find some stale bread we can spare.'

'Can you run them down to the Duck pond Bill?'

'No need.' Harry pitched in. 'We can walk. It will be good exercise.'

'OK, sounds like a plan.' Jean replied opening cupboards and starting to fill a brown bag with bread from the back of the bread bin.

They were soon off on their adventure, with Laddie following them. They took PC's football and spent most of the time kicking it to each other as they walked down the long path to the pond which was at the furthest edge of the farm. Every now and then the dog would chase the ball, but he seemed unsure what to do with it.

A small brook ran into the pond and they played at the edge of that, floating small sticks down the brook and seeing whose stick reached the pond first. Laddie would bark at the sticks and the boys discovered that if they threw a stick Laddie would scamper off and bring it back without a problem. Harry suggested to PC that maybe Laddie had not seen a ball before.

As soon as the ducks saw the boys they started paddling towards them and the boys threw pieces of bread out into the pond, as far as they could, and laughed as the ducks flapped and chased each other around the pond in an effort to get to as much bread as possible. They didn't notice the ball roll down into the brook and in an instant the brook had taken it out into the middle of the pond.

'My ball,' shouted PC.

He took off his shoes and socks and started to wade in, but the pond was too deep, and the ball was getting further and further out of reach.

Laddie seemed to understand what was happening and jumped into the water, splashing PC as he went past the boy. He headed out into the pond and circled behind the ball, pushing it back towards the boys and the edge of the pond. PC gratefully collected the ball from Laddie and waded back out of the pond, followed by the dog. When they were all on the shore Laddie shook himself dry, ensuring the boys got soaked.

They didn't care.

Both boys stroked the dog and thanked him for fetching their football.

PC picked up his socks and shoes and barefoot he walked with Harry, who carried the ball, and Laddie until they found a sunny patch by a wall where they sat while they all dried out. Laddie sat between the boys and was instantly asleep and lulled by the warmth and the presence of the dog, both boys were soon asleep too.

That's where Bill found them. The sound of the tractor had woken them, but they were still half asleep when Bill pulled up alongside them.

'Come on sleepy heads, lunch is ready.'

The boys clambered on to the trailer and Bill helped Laddie on to his lap before they turned and headed back for the farmhouse and another hearty ploughman's lunch. PC couldn't get enough of the pickle and cheese Jean served them.

That afternoon Bill took them to the field with the cows and the boys watched while he milked the small herd, tipping the milk into a churn which they helped him carry on to the trailer. He explained that Jean would make butter with most of the milk and the rest would go into their tea or be used for rice puddings. He explained how they were almost self-sufficient, particularly in the summer though it can be tough in the winter.

Supper that night was chicken, with mash and root vegetables. Jean explained how one of their chickens had stopped laying so she had to go. However, she had done the deed while the boys were out milking the cows with Bill so they wouldn't see how she killed and plucked the bird. She was a little sad as it had been one of her favourite birds.

However, the boys still enjoyed their supper and seeing their smiling faces and the clean plates cheered her up. After tea they had Apple and loganberry crumble with warm custard before Bill went out to stretch his legs.

While Bill pottered in the garden after tea and the boys helped with the dishes, Jean explained how they couldn't have children. Bill had always wanted a son to inherit the farm but it wouldn't happen now and they were destined to have to pass the farm on to one of her siblings children or sell it when they got older. As she washed, they could see the tears running down her face and Harry gave her a hug and put his head on her shoulder. There was nothing they could think to say.

'Do you want to stay a bit longer?' Jean asked once the dishes were dried and put away.

'We can't Jean.' Harry said a little reluctantly. He had loved the farm and felt for the couple. He also knew he had no parents to go home too.

'We need to get back, people will be worried and PC's parents are waiting for him.'

'I know luv, just liked having you around.'

'Can we come back and visit one day?' PC asked.

'Course you can Luv.' Jean replied.

‘Thank you so much for looking after us.’ Harry said with genuine warmth.

‘Come here,’ Jean said holding her arms out. She wrapped her arms around them both and they hugged her back.

Before bed that night Bill sat down with them in the snug, as Jean called it, with a map of the Southwest and showed them how best to get to Weymouth. They drank horlicks while the radio played quietly behind them as he took them through the various options and the quickest and safest way to make the journey.

His suggestion was that they head for Chard then pass through Axminster on their way to Charmouth and Lyme Regis. From there they could follow the coast to Weymouth via Bridport and Chesil Beach.

‘You won’t believe Chesil Beach when you see it,’ he said, ‘but if I were you, I wouldn’t walk along it, keep to the land side. The pebbles will be harder on your feet and you will need to double back on yourselves at the end to get to Weymouth Harbour.

I must go to Corfe tomorrow, so I’ll take you there and Jean is going to make you some chicken sandwiches to keep you going. He reached into his pocket and gave the boys a pound note each. ‘We don’t have much but please take this and make sure you don’t starve. And come back and see us one day. There will always be a bed for you here.’

Without getting up he leaned forward and shook the boy’s hands in turn and then shooed them off to bed. As they stood up, he looked up at them.

‘Get some sleep boys, you may not get to sleep in a proper bed for a few days. See you in the morning.’

The boys went off to bed and Bill lay back on the sofa and cried a few tears for the son he never had. Jean came in to join him and seeing his tears, led him off to bed.

Next morning after a bit of a lie in and another hearty breakfast the boys were given their chicken sandwiches and a bag of apples before they said a tearful farewell to Jean. They climbed on to the trailer and headed off with Bill towards Corfe. They were soon on the main road and heading south at a leisurely 20 miles an hour.

After 15 minutes of driving through the beautiful Somerset countryside, in the sunshine, they arrived in Corfe. Bill had to collect some hay from a farm near Corfe so he turned off the road and pulled up in front of the White Hart Inn so the boys could jump off the trailer.

He turned the tractor engine off and came around to talk to the boys.

'Well, have you got all your things?' Bill asked.

'Yes Bill.' Harry replied for both. They stood there with their kit bags over their shoulders and PC had his precious football under his arm.

Bill gave them each a hug in turn.

'Now head on down the Yarcombe road until you get to a junction. Take the left turn to Chard, you'll see a signpost if they have put them back. Once you get to Chard go South to the coast. It's about 12 miles to Chard so if you don't dawdle, you'll get there in time to find somewhere to stay the night.'

'Thanks Bill.' PC responded. 'We'll never forget what you have done for us.'

They both hugged Bill one last time then headed back to the road and turned right towards Yarcombe. As they turned the corner they looked back and waved. Bill waved back, smiling through the tears.

'A la Perchoine.' PC shouted. 'We'll see you again.'

With that he dropped his ball and kicked it down the road. Both boys ran after it and disappeared from view.

Bill smiled to himself. *I am sure we will see you both again,* he thought, as he turned the key and started off towards the farm to make his collection. He had loved the last couple of days.

Harry got to the ball first and passed it back to PC and off they went down the road to Chard passing the ball backwards and forwards to each other as they made their way down a virtually deserted road. Occasionally they would stop to pick some early season blackberries and take an occasional drink from a stream. After they had turned off the Yarcombe road, they walked and ran, kicking the ball for about an hour before deciding it was time for a rest and for lunch. They climbed over a gate into a field and sat in the sun, with their backs against a wall, to eat their chicken sandwiches. They followed that with an apple from Jeans orchard and chatted about how lovely the couple were and how they would arrange to go back and visit, when they were a little older.

Gradually the conversation slowed as they got sleepy and soon both were fast asleep.

PC had a dream that he was in a lovely warm bathroom with hot water running and a wet flannel was gently rubbing his skin. He awoke with a start as he realised the wet feeling on his face wasn't a dream. A huge cow towered over him, licking his face while another in the herd had a giant pee. PC screamed out loud, startling the cow and waking Harry.

'Flaming heck.' Harry cried. 'Let's get out of here.'

The boys stood up, causing the cows to move back with a start. They grabbed their gear and the ball and ran back to the gate and quickly clambered out of the field.

'Where did they come from?' PC asked as they jumped down into the road.

The answer lay in the road as there was a trail of mud and cow manure running down the road into a gate on the other side. The cows must have been moved by a farmer from one field to the one the boys were in.

The boys ran down the road, stepping over the cow manure, until they had passed the other gate and had a clean road ahead of them.

They reached a crossroads and took the road south continuing their journey through the Blackdown Hills.

They soon reached Combe St Nicholas and attracted little attention as they passed through the village, pausing to look at the ancient church of St Nicholas which had been the centre piece of the town for over 700 years. They spotted a sweet shop as they walked through the village and bought a bag of toffees before carrying on towards Wadeford and Chard. When they reached Wadeford they knew they were getting close to Chard.

They always picked up the ball as they went through the villages and did so again in Wadeford. They passed the Haymakers Inn and headed out of the village. They didn't have a watch between them but knew the afternoon was fast turning to evening. It took them just under an hour to get to Chard. It would have been quicker if Harry hadn't kicked the ball a bit too hard over a hedge. The boys had to find a way into the field and then get the ball out of some brambles. It took them a while but eventually they prised it out, earning a few scratches along the way. They also found a few blackberries in the process to assuage their growing hunger.

After a while they were on the outskirts of Chard and started to look for a place they could spend the night.

Walking through the town the smell of cooking seemed to be everywhere and the boys realised just how hungry they were.

They kept walking toward the south and spotted the Parish Church of Saint Mary's.

'Maybe we can sleep in there?' PC suggested.

'Good idea.' Harry nodded and the pair turned off the path and headed up towards the church. As they walked towards the Church, they could see a light on inside and could hear an organ playing. The clock told them it was just after 7pm and as it wasn't a Sunday, they were pretty sure there wouldn't be a service taking place. They crept through the door and peeked into the main body of the Church. They were impressed by the two rows of tall columns and the lovely stained glass window above the altar. In the far-right hand corner they could see the organ and a girl with long wavy black hair sat playing the organ.

She seemed to be in a world of her own and was unaware of the boys watching her.

Enthralled they took a seat amongst the rows of wooden pews and watched as she played a range of hymns, a few of which the boys recognised.

'She's good eh!'

The boys nearly jumped out of their skins as the voice was right behind them. They hadn't noticed the vicar come in and sit in the row behind them.

They turned and saw a smiling grey-haired man in ordinary clothes, but wearing a dog collar, looking at them. 'She's my daughter,' he added proudly.

‘She’s very good,’ PC replied a little nervously.

‘She is that,’ Harry added. ‘Guess we’d best get going.’

‘Hang on boys,’ the Vicar interrupted as they both got up to leave. ‘Where are you from?’

‘We’re from the Channel Islands sir,’ PC replied, ‘and we are on our way home.’

‘Well then I guess you need somewhere to sleep tonight. Would you like to stay with us in the Manse?’

Neither boys knew what a Manse was but they both nodded enthusiastically.

They waited until the Vicars daughter finished playing the hymn she was practicing and before she could start another one, he called out to her.

‘Norma!’, he called out.

She turned around and beamed a beautiful smile which lit up the church. That rapidly changed to curiosity as she saw her Dad sitting there with the two boys.

‘We have guests for tea,’ he added.

Norma skipped down the Church to join her Dad and the boys and they all shook hands a little awkwardly.

‘Come on you lot,’ the Vicar said, getting up and heading out of the church. ‘Let’s eat before the dog beats us to it.’

Norma headed off first and the two boys followed along a little unsure.

The Vicar held the door open until they had all filed out of the church then he flicked a few switches, plunging the church into darkness and locked the door. They all then headed along a path to the Manse which was in the same grounds as the church.

As soon as the Vicar opened the door of the manse, the smell was amazing and the boys were reminded just how hungry they were. They dropped their bags and the ball inside the porch and took their shoes off, as the Vicar and Norma had done. Norma led them into the kitchen. The boys were given chairs at the table and an extra two plates were set on the table which had been laid out for two.

Soon a wonderful meal of stew and dumplings was being served up. Harry was about to tuck in when the vicar cleared his throat rather loudly.

'Let's say grace before we eat boys,' he said smiling.

He held Norma's hand and with his eyes closed said a prayer.

'Dear Lord, for what we are about to receive make us truly grateful and Lord, thank you for bringing Harry and PC safely to us and ensuring we are able to help them in their journey home. Amen.'

Norma echoed the Amen and the boys followed suit.

'Tuck in everyone,' the Vicar said with a smile and soon they were all enjoying their evening meal.

As they ate the vicar teased the boy's story out of them and how they wanted to go home together rather than be split up. He was worried when he heard about their health issues but they both seemed well enough. He hadn't noticed PC limping or any issues with Harry's health so had concluded they were well on the mend. In fact, they both looked amazingly healthy with a nice colour to their skins and rosy cheeks which indicated long days spent outdoors. They spoke about the farm and how kind Bill and Jean had been to them.

The Vicar introduced himself as John Moore and explained that he had been the local vicar here for the last 5 years but seemed reticent to say much about himself being more interested in the boy's adventures. When he heard that Harry's father had been killed at Dunkirk a deep sadness seemed to come over him.

Supper concluded with a wonderful apple and black currant crumble which Norma proudly announced she had made. After the dishes were done they retired to the lounge and John put on the Home Service on the radio which was playing Flotsam's Follies, while Norma made a cup of tea for them all.

As they sat the boys looked around the room. It was a big room, far bigger than anything they had experienced in a house. It had a high ceiling with a mini chandelier hanging from an ornate ceiling rose. The walls were papered with a flowery design and two big wooden cabinets with glass fronts were along two of the walls. One was full of books while the other was full of china, glass and several photos. Over the fireplace, with its fire all laid but unlit were a couple of photographs which caught their attention. One was a family group with the vicar and Norma easily identifiable along with a woman, who the boys assumed was the vicar's wife and two young men in uniform. The other photo was the two boys on their own, again both in uniform smiling at the camera and looking very smart. They could have been twins.

The boys were curious but too polite to ask.

They drank their tea and answered question the couple had about Guernsey and Jersey before the vicar suggested it was time for bed.

'I'll go and prepare a room for the boys, Norma, will you make some cocoa?'

‘Yes father,’ she replied and headed off to the kitchen as John made his way upstairs.

The boys looked at each other.

‘They seem nice,’ PC offered.

‘They do,’ Harry replied. ‘I wonder where Norma’s Mum and brothers are?’

Norma came back into the room at that moment to ask if they wanted sugar in their cocoa and heard the question.

‘They’re dead. My brothers were killed in the war, both in the retreat to Dunkirk while fighting for the BEF and Mum died of a broken heart about 6 months later.’

She went across to the family photo.

‘This is Mark and this one is Nigel,’ she said as she pointed out her older brothers. ‘They were twins and joined up together.’

‘Mum was a bit older than Dad and was always a bit frail, especially after I was born. When the news came of their loss, she was inconsolable for weeks and seemed to waste away over the following months. Dad has been a rock and we look after each other.’

‘Do you want sugar in your cocoa?’ Norma asked after she put the photo back on the mantelpiece.

‘No thank you,’ the boys replied quietly, still taking in all that had been said.

‘I’m so sorry,’ Harry added thoughtfully.

Norma smiled at him and went back to the kitchen to finish off making their drinks.

‘She’s lovely,’ Harry whispered to PC.

PC smiled back.

After they had enjoyed their drinks and John had come back downstairs to announce that their room was ready, the boys grabbed their bags, leaving the ball in the porch, and headed up to the bedroom. They were given the chance to use the bathroom first. They found pyjamas and towels laid out on the two single beds and after getting changed for bed washed their faces and cleaned their teeth before climbing into bed.

When they were settled in bed the vicar popped his head around the door.

‘Goodnight boys.’

‘Goodnight,’ they said hesitantly.

‘Just call me John,’ he said smiling.

‘Goodnight John,’ they replied in unison.

As he shut the door Norma was standing behind him. She gave him a hug knowing what he was thinking. Tears flowed down his face and she could feel his body shaking as he wept.

‘It’s like they’ve come home at last,’ he whispered in her ear.

‘I know Dad, I know.’ She said with tears in her eyes.

‘Get some sleep and we can see how we can help them tomorrow.’

‘Thanks Love,’ he said and kissed her forehead before they headed to their own rooms and the lights in the house went out one by one.

*****

Next morning the boys were woken up by the light streaming through the thin bedroom curtains. Harry jumped out of bed and looked out to see what he could see. In front of them was the church, the graveyard, the town of Chard and in the distance, he could see trees and fields. It was a beautiful day with the blue sky dotted with the occasional fluffy cloud. People were walking up and down the road outside the church grounds going about their business, walking to work, shopping or taking the dog for a walk. A few vans drove around, and a lone horse and cart clip clopped its way past the graveyard laden with beer barrels, no doubt heading for the pub Harry could see across the road.

'Come on sleepy head,' Harry called to PC. 'Time to get up and see what adventures we can get up to today.'

PC stirred and sat up rubbing his eyes. He could see Harry staring out of the window and for the first time had a good look around the room they were in. He had been so tired last night his head had barely hit the pillow before he was sound asleep. It was a big room compared to what he was used to. High ceilings, two windows, a fireplace and a large wooden bookshelf. A basin and jug sat on a wooden unit full of shelves and next to the bowl were rows of toy soldiers. It was a very male room.

He got out of bed and looked at the books. There were dozens of them with adventure stories in the majority. Moby Dick, Treasure Island, Gulliver's Travels sat there amongst many history books, several based on the Boer War and the Great War. This was definitely a boy's room. Many more toy soldiers sat on the shelves in front of the books, the most striking being a mounted figurine of Napoleon on his famous white horse, Marengo, waving a sword. It sat in front a set of Napoleonic books including a large book about the Battle of Waterloo. Everything was very neat and tidy.

There were a couple of photos on the Mantelpiece and he went over to look at those. The photos were the two boys. One saw them posing in football kit, obviously after winning a match as they were all muddy but smiling and holding a trophy between them. The other was them in military uniform, looking as if they were off to war.

PC felt a tear in his eye as he thought of the boys living happily in this house and enjoying their lives before having their futures taken away from them during the war. Harry came over and saw that PC looked upset.

'What's the matter,' he said putting an arm around his friends' shoulder.

'Look at them Harry, so happy and carefree, just like us and now they are dead. Imagine what John must be thinking with us here, in their beds and wearing their pyjamas.'

The two boys were quiet for a moment.

'Best be careful what we say then,' Harry commented. 'Let's not talk about the war and his boys. Come on let's get dressed and see what's for breakfast.'

Ten minutes later the boys were downstairs and enjoying toast and jam with John and his daughter.

'Did you sleep well?' Norma asked.

'Like a log,' Harry said, smiling.

PC could see Harry liked Norma and smiled to himself.

'What do you plan to do today?' John asked.

'Guess we should be heading on towards home,' PC said after a moment's thought. 'The weather is good, and we need to get to Axminster and then the south coast.'

‘Maybe you could stay a day, I am sure it wouldn’t make that much difference,’ Norma suggested.

Harry smiled and PC thought for a moment.

‘I suppose,’ he finally decided. ‘If that’s OK with you sir?’

‘Of course,’ John replied happily. ‘What would you like to do while you are here? The weather looks great, we could wander out for the day and have a picnic.’

‘What do you think Norma, Chardstock?’

‘Oh yes Dad, that would be fun.’

The boys had no idea where Chardstock was but were happy to go along with the Father and Daughter and before long a picnic was packed, and they were off on another adventure.

They left the Manse and headed up Church Street and Tatworth Street before heading into the fields. They were following a well-trodden footpath which took them south towards Chardstock and the fields of the Blackdown Hills. The path led them alongside streams, over stiles and through fields, often filled with cows or sheep. In one field some men in grey uniforms were cutting hay by hand and one shouted to them as they passed.

‘Guten Morgen!’

‘Guten Morgen,’ the Vicar shouted back. He explained to the boys that they were German prisoners of war waiting to be shipped home and were being utilised by the farmers to help with the harvest. The farmers were short of workers because so many men had been involved in the war and were yet to come home.

The boys looked over and many of the men had stopped work to look at the group, several of whom were whistling and waving at them. The boys quickly realised it was Norma who was the main target of their attention and her father positioned himself between her and them protectively as they skirted the field. A guard in uniform carrying a rifle was soon on the scene encouraging them back to work and slowly they got back to their efforts, scything and collecting the hay into stacks using pitchforks.

PC wondered why they seemed so obedient bearing in mind they had 'weapons' in their hands and seemed to outnumber the guard by a hundred to one. He kept that thought to himself and decided to ask the question when the time was right.

Soon they were over another stile and the prisoners were left to their work. More beautiful scenery appeared in front of them and soon a tower came into sight, it was the tower of Chardstock parish church. Before long they were in the village which the boys had to agree was very beautiful. They passed the George Inn with its thatched roof and headed up to a plateau which had excellent views. They found a corner of a field and John declared it was lunch time.

Norma and the boys got to work spreading out a blanket and laying out the food and drink. It was a veritable feast. They enjoyed glasses of lemonade, sandwiches and fruit. A bar of chocolate was found at the bottom of the basket and they all savoured a piece to finish off their dinner.

PC had brought his ball with them and soon they were having a kick about. The vicar joined in as Norma packed the blanket away and put the debris of lunch back into the basket. She then joined in gamely, kicking the ball to the boys and her Dad as best she could. She admitted she had never kicked a ball before, but everyone was happy that she was joining in and at least having a go. Harry thought she did 'really well' much to PC's amusement.

John had also brought along a small brownie camera and Norma and the boys were soon posing for photos and she took one of the Vicar with the boys, him holding the ball.

They had been on the plateau for about an hour when a pair of spitfires flew low over the hills and headed south towards the coast. They all cheered as they flew overhead. The war might be over, but evidence of the conflict was everywhere.

They sat down to lemonade and PC asked the question that had been puzzling him.

'John, why don't those prisoners run away? They could easily overpower the guards and make an escape.'

John took a sip of his lemonade then replied.

'I am no expert, but I guess now the war is over, most of them just want to get back home and behaving themselves is the best way for them to achieve that. Besides if they did do something stupid like that there is a fair chance they would be shot by the guards or the people sent to recapture them.'

PC took that in for a moment then replied.

'I want to go home too, and I guess I would do everything I could to get there as quickly as possible.'

'Yes,' John replied. 'But you also need to make sure you get home safely.'

He gave a knowing smile to the boys and they both nodded.

'Just promise me you won't do anything silly or dangerous on the way back.' Norma added. 'I would love to see you both again in a while, maybe visit you.'

She spoke to them both but was looking at Harry, who immediately blushed like a ripe Braeburn apple.

'We'll be careful,' PC replied smiling, as Harry tried to compose himself.

'Let's get back,' John said, getting up and grabbing the picnic basket. 'Then we can talk about the rest of your journey.'

The four of them made their way back to Chard but John took them back by a slightly different route. The scenery was beautiful, but he managed to avoid passing the prisoners, no doubt to spare his daughter from their attentions.

That evening they dined on sausages and mash, the vicar proudly announcing they were his own home-grown potatoes.

Harry had commented that they were lovely but not as nice as Jersey Royals. They all laughed at that.

While they were washing up the topic of their journey home was raised by John.

Harry explained that the idea was to head south to Charmouth and then follow the coast to Weymouth. John got out an ancient map of the south of England and they agreed on the best route to take. The next town to aim for was Axminster which started a brief history lesson from John on the carpet industry in that town.

He spotted PC yawning at one point and then mentioned that they had quite a good football team who were nicknamed, the Tigers, which they found much more interesting. He explained that one of his sons had played for them for a season before the war. The boys chose not to respond, trying to avoid saying anything wrong.

They had listened to the news on the radio and Tuesday Serenade was just beginning which signaled it was time for bed. It was agreed the boys would head out after breakfast the next morning.

As they got up from the table, John stood and shook their hands.

'It has been a pleasure having you stay with us,' he said quite formally. 'Please keep in touch and let us know that you have got home safely. It would be lovely to see you both again at some point in the next few years.'

The boys both promised to keep in touch and left the father and daughter in their living room and went up to bed.

Once they were both in bed, PC whispered to Harry. 'You really like her don't you.'

'Yes, I do,' he replied sleepily. 'I think I might be married to her one day.'

PC smiled to himself and he heard Harry's breathing change as he dropped off to sleep.

Maybe you will, he thought. Maybe you will.

Chapter Four

Sister Christine had been shocked to hear that the boys had disappeared from their beds overnight. As soon as the morning rounds were completed, she called Nurse Catherine into her small office and for a while they discussed how it was possible they could break out, bearing in mind the ward was supervised all night.

'We'll look into it in more detail later,' Christine said with a big sigh. 'I reckon they must have had some help. The question now is what do we do next, we can't leave them wandering about out there on their own.'

'Will they be alright?' Catherine asked. 'Physically I mean. It just seems too early for them, especially Peter to be walking too far.'

'My thoughts exactly,' Christine replied. 'I need to talk to the Doctor to find out what he thinks.'

'Where do you think they have gone?' Catherine asked.

'That's the million-dollar question,' Christine replied. 'My guess is that because the Doctor said they would be separated, they decided to make their own way home together. That begs the question which way would they go and how did they think they could find their way and keep themselves fed and watered until they got home?'

They both stared at each other for a moment. They had no answer.

'Right, let's make a plan,' Sister Christine said with purpose. 'I'll go and talk to the Doctor and see if he feels Peter or Harry are at any risk. You go and see if you can find us a jeep and a driver who knows the area who has some time this afternoon to help us with a search of the area. I'll clear our schedules for after lunch and we will head out and see if we can spot them anywhere.'

They both got up with a flurry and headed off to carry out their agreed tasks.

Sister Christine found Major Bill Cornelius in the canteen. She was particularly worried about PC and as Major Bill had set PC's leg, she felt he was the best person to talk to about him. She quickly appraised him of the situation. He too was amazed at how the boys had managed to get out of the hospital and more so how they escaped from the grounds, considering the guards manned the gate 24 hours a day.

'I would have been happy if he had been resting for another week,' he replied to her question. 'All I can hope he is being sensible and doesn't spend too much time walking each day, gentle exercise is good but if he starts running and jumping, he could undo all the good work of the last few weeks. In a worst-case scenario, he could open up the break and even get an infection. If that happens, without treatment he could lose his leg!'

'That's useful,' Christine replied. 'I am organising a vehicle so we can try and see if we can find them. I think the quicker we can get them back the better.'

'I agree with that,' Major Bill replied looking over the top of his glasses. He reached for his coffee cup and added. 'If you need any help requisitioning the jeep, just use my name. Happy hunting.'

With that Sister Christine got up and with a smile of gratitude left the canteen and headed back to the ward. Now she had to sort out the rotas so she and Nurse Catherine could take a few hours that afternoon to try and find where the boys had gone.

By 12 noon the jeep was organised and the two friends were changed into their civvies. The driver was a GI Corporal called

Karl who came from New York. He had been with the Hospital for a year since being wounded on D-Day. He had been with the 90th Infantry Division when they went ashore on Utah beach but had been badly wounded and had taken many months to recover. Rather than going back to New York he had volunteered to stay and help out at the Hospital. He would tell anyone who listened that he owed his health and his life to the Taunton Hospital and the West Country fresh air.

They climbed in the back of the jeep and Karl turned to them and with a big cheesy smile and New York drawl said, "Where to girls?'

'If you were driving to Weymouth, which way would you go?' Christine asked Karl.

'Well Chrissy,' Karl replied using a name Christine hated. 'I would head to Ilminster, then Crewkerne, then take the road to Dorchester then on down to Weymouth.'

'Sounds a good place to start,' Catherine replied. 'What do you think Christine?' She emphasised her name to make the point as she knew Christine hated being called Chrissy.

'Let's go!' Christine replied, pointing to the hospital gates and soon they were whizzing through Taunton and off into the countryside - in completely the wrong direction.

Later that afternoon they returned from their unsuccessful tour of the roads around Crewkerne including a visit to Cricket St Thomas. They had come back via Chard, having sped through the town convinced they were in the wrong area. Further up the road to Taunton they had passed a barn and a distant farmhouse and if they could have seen through the stone walls surrounding the farmers' fields, they would have seen the two young runaways, enjoying a laze in the afternoon sun. The reality was the boys were closer to Taunton than they thought.

That evening as they worked a later shift, Sister Christine and Nurse Catherine poured over a map of the area, given to them by Karl. They tried to put themselves in the shoes of the boys and work out which way they would have travelled on foot. The reality was there were a number of ways they could have made their way towards Weymouth and it would take a stroke of enormous luck for them to find the right direction and eventually find PC and Harry, but they weren't about to give up.

'I think if I was walking to Weymouth I might want to get to the south coast as quick as I could and head this way.' Christine suggested pointing a pen towards the small town of Axminster.

Catherine nodded in agreement. 'I think you're right, especially if I didn't know the roads very well.'

The friends poured over the map for a few more minutes and then decided to head to Axminster next time they got some time off together, it seemed a logical place to start. Christine made a note to try and get some transport organised with Karl, but all that would have to wait as they had a full day of work ahead of them and little chance to reorganise their rotas, particular as some of the nurses were now being shipped back to the US and staff numbers were short.

They just didn't have enough resources to mount a full-scale search.

Chapter Five

The next morning the boys were up bright and early. They were washed and dressed before 8am then enjoyed a breakfast of eggs, bacon and sausages. They all helped with the dishes before the boys went back upstairs to clean their teeth and visit the loo before packing and heading downstairs to say goodbye.

John shook their hands again and wished them a safe journey, he also handed them a couple of bags with ham sandwiches and apples 'to see them through the day'. Norma hugged PC and then Harry. Harry for a tiny bit longer. PC noted she whispered something in Harry's ear as they hugged.

'Now, you know which way you are going?' he asked them.

'Yes sir,' PC replied confidently.

'Well just in case I have drawn out the route on this piece of paper and also included our address on the back so you can let us know that you have got home safely.'

He had made two copies and gave one to each of the boys who tucked the bits of paper into their bags.

They walked to the front door, PC picking up his football from the porch on the way. On a whim he asked John and Norma to sign his football which they duly did.

'Thank you for everything,' Harry said as they walked out of the house. 'We'll see you again.'

'Bye!' they both shouted as they broke into a gentle run and headed out of the grounds of the Manse, turning for one last wave as they went out of the gate and into the road. Turning south they were soon heading out of the town on to the Axminster road which would take them to their next target. As soon as they were out of the town PC dropped the ball and gave it a kick down the road. Harry had been very quiet up till then and PC could have sworn that he had noticed a tear in his eye as they left Chard behind them.

However, the sight of the ball rolling down the hill was enough to spur them both into action and before long they were chasing it south as they made their way towards Axminster kicking it to each other when the road was clear. It was clear for most of the time with only a few military trucks disturbing their journey south. The whole journey was only about 7 miles and they made good time as they were jogging most of the way. They soon came across Weycroft and a beautiful stone bridge which crossed the River Axe.

They stood and looked over the bridge for a while, enjoying the sight of swans and ducks swimming around the arches of the bridge.

Harry was holding the ball and suddenly stood back and threw the ball to PC. 'Header,' he shouted, and lobbed to ball to PC. PC turned but wasn't quick enough and the ball hit his shoulder and bounced on the parapet of the bridge. They both made a dive for it as it rolled along the parapet of the bridge before dropping over the other side and landing in the river. The two friends rushed to the other side just in time to see the ball float out from under the bridge and head off down the river.

'Quick,' yelled PC, 'let's follow it.'

The boys rushed back the way they had come and at the end of the bridge spotted a path alongside the river and rushed down it. PC had noticed his leg was starting to ache so slowed down as they took the slope to the river. They could see the ball sailing along in the centre of the river but the stream was slow, so they soon caught up with it. The river swung away to the right and started to slow even further but the ball stubbornly stayed in the middle where the flow was quickest. At one point they tried throwing stones at it but after one splash sent the ball a bit further away, they thought better of that idea.

Soon the river turned to the left again and PC spotted a small island up ahead where the river narrowed quite considerably. He found a branch and rushed ahead to the narrow point and waited until the ball approached and reached out to try and stop it. Harry held his hand so he could lean out further, but they were still a couple of feet short. PC leaned out a bit further and just as he did that Harry's foot slipped and they both fell into the water.

Harry scrambled back out quickly while PC got a real soaking. He stood there, thoroughly soaked, but still had the presence of mind to turn and get the ball back, using the branch which was floating alongside him. He trudged back on to the path, the ball under one arm with the kit bag containing all his worldly goods still on his back.

Harry looked at PC, completely bedraggled and splattered in mud, and burst out laughing.

PC burst out laughing too. Harry was wet up to his waist and covered in mud. He threw Harry the ball who promptly fell over backwards on to the grass.

PC lay down alongside him and together they laughed until there was no more laughter inside of them.

Exhausted they lay there in the sun allowing the heat of the day to dry them off.

'What did Norma say to you?' PC asked.

Harry smiled and looked at his friend. 'She said she really liked me.'

'That's nice,' was all PC could think to say.

They lay there for a while, lulled by the warmth and the sound of the running water.

Finally, Harry got up and suggested they get going. PC was almost dry and seemed happy to continue their journey. His leg seemed to be feeling a bit better.

'Which way?' PC asked as he scrambled to his feet, wiping off some of the dried mud with his hands.

Harry thought for a minute. 'Let's follow the river,' he suggested. 'It should take us towards the sea and Axminster.'

'OK,' PC agreed, 'but my leg is aching a bit so let's walk for a while.

'Are you sure you are OK to carry on? Harry asked concerned for his friend.

'I'm fine but let's take it easy.'

With that, they got going, PC kicked the ball ahead of him down the path. Harry chased after it and proceeded to do all the running as PC walked the journey. They carried on like that until they saw the sign for Axminster.

A narrow path led off to their left so PC picked up the ball and they headed that way, determined to get back on track. They had eaten a few wild blackberries on the way and their tummies were beginning to grumble as they had been forced to share Harry's sandwiches, PC's being ruined when he fell in the river. All they had from Peter's bag that could be salvaged was the apple, which he had been eaten after a quick wash in the river.

Within half an hour they were crossing a railway line on the outskirts of the town and from there they passed an old building which turned out to be a brush factory. From there they headed up the hill towards the centre of Axminster, not sure what to do next. At the top of the hill they passed along a small lane which brought them out opposite the church in the centre of town. For a while they sat on the wall surrounding the church grounds and looked enviously at the George Hotel and the warmth that emanated from the hotel. Harry's tummy rumbled at that moment and PC joked it sounded like distant thunder. They both laughed.

'It would be lovely to have a nice meal in there,' PC said, stating the obvious.

Harry just shrugged his shoulders. 'I don't think that's going to happen,' he added after a pause. 'It looks very expensive.'

The town was quiet as they sat bouncing the ball, enjoying watching the occasional horse and cart clip clop past where they sat. They were about to start a kick about when Harry noticed a man waving at them from the George Hotel.

'Is he waving at us?' Harry said, pointing off towards the hotel.

'Looks like it,' PC replied. 'What have we done wrong?' He added, immediately on the defensive.

'Lads, come here,' the man shouted and beckoned them towards the hotel.

A little reluctantly the boys made their way across to the hotel and the man pointed to the carriage entrance and told them to go in.

The boys walked into the dark entrance where the carriages dropped off the guests and PC stepped into a pile of horse manure.

'Urghhh,' he cried. 'That's disgusting.'

'Exactly.' The man commented with a hint of a laugh. 'How would you like to earn yourselves some supper lads?'

'What do we have to do?' Harry asked thinking he knew the answer.

The man reached inside the door and produced a shovel and bucket. ‘Can you clean this lot up before our evening guests arrive?’

‘Where do we put it?’ PC asked.

‘Cook will use it for soup,’ the man said smiling. He saw the look of shock on the boys faces and burst out laughing.

‘Just joking for goodness sake. There’s a midden around the back of the hotel, you can dump it there.’

‘My names George by the way,’ he said, holding out his hand. The boys shook his hand in turn.

‘Is this your Hotel then?’ PC asked.

‘No such luck I’m afraid,’ George replied. ‘Just a coincidence I’ve got the same name.’

‘Try and get the cobbles as clean as you can lads and supper is on me.’

With that George headed back into the hotel and the boys looked at each other and the horse manure that surrounded them.

‘Well this won’t put food in our tummies!’ Harry stated, grabbing the bucket. ‘You shovel and I’ll take the buckets of horse shit around the back.’

PC burst out laughing. ‘What?’ Harry asked.

‘You said shit.’ PC whispered with a big smile on his face. ‘I have never heard you swear before.’

‘My Dad used to say it all the time.’ Harry mused, obviously thinking wistfully of his father. A sad look came over his face and PC put his arm around his shoulder.

‘If my Dad was alive, I wouldn’t be shovelling shit.’ Harry blurted out and the boys laughed again at the use of the word and the mood changed instantly.

PC grabbed the shovel and gingerly started to scrape the horse manure off the cobbles, dropping each shovel load into the big bucket. Three shovel loads were usually enough to fill the bucket and PC would rest while Harry went around the back of the hotel to the midden to dump the manure. This routine went on for about an hour before they stood back and admired their work.

‘Do you think that’s clean enough?’ PC asked.

‘I reckon,’ Harry replied. ‘I’ll go and find George.’

With that Harry went through the door that George had used and disappeared.

About two minutes later there was a bit of a commotion the other side of the door and next thing Harry came flying out, ably assisted on his journey by George’s boot.

‘For goodness sake boys, you can’t come in here smelling like that, get yourselves cleaned up and put on some decent clothes and then you can come in here for your meal.’

‘But we haven’t got anywhere to get cleaned up and these are virtually all the clothes we have.’ PC tried to explain.

George looked at their desperate faces and took a moment to have a think. He had a look around to see if they had done the job well and then made a decision.

‘Tell you what,’ he said with a smile, ‘you go down to the river and wash your face and hands and get as much of the muck off your shoes as you can. Meet me around the back of the hotel by the midden in half an hour and I’ll bring you out some food.’

The boys smiled back and headed off down the hill to the river, they quickly took off their shoes and gave them a good rinse in the slow moving water and then washed their hands and faces before drying them on their jumpers and heading back up the hill. PC kicked his ball up the hill and then raced to stop it as it rolled back down. By the time they got back to the George they were quite tired.

They went around the back and sat on the edge of a horse trough next to the midden and waited. After a few minutes, true to his word, George appeared. He made them hold out their hands for inspection and told them to wait a minute and went back into the hotel. A minute or two went by before he came back out with two bowls of steaming lamb stew with dumplings. This was accompanied by two big chunks of bread on a separate plate, brought out by one of the waiters, as well as a couple of jugs of local cider.

‘Here you go boys,’ George said with a smile. ‘Your reward for a job well done.’

‘Thank you so much.’ Harry replied with a big smile and soon they were both tucking in.

George watched for a minute as the boys ate their meal. ‘I’ll be back for the empties in half an hour,’ he said as he left them to it.

‘This is great,’ PC muttered with a mouth full of bread. Harry simply nodded as he continued to scoff down his meal.

They were soon drinking the cider George had given them and suddenly Harry just burst out laughing. PC smiled as we all do when other people laugh and soon, he was laughing too. 'What's so funny.' PC managed to blurt out.

'I don't know,' Harry replied, tears rolling down his cheeks.

They finished off their cider and were suddenly very sleepy. The boys carefully piled their empty bowls and glasses down beside them then slid down to sit with their backs to the horse trough. Within minutes they were sound asleep. Tiredness, full bellies and alcohol creating the prefect soporific.

A few minutes later George came out to get their empty dishes and found them both sound asleep leaning on each other. He quietly walked over and carefully picked up their empty dishes, which looked as if they had been licked clean, and took them inside. He came back with a woollen blanket and gently placed it over the boys as the sun was starting to set and he was worried they might get cold.

'I'll give them half an hour,' he thought to himself and went back in to continue his work.

It was around 6.30pm before George went back out and he gently shook each boy awake. Both were quite disorientated when they woke up and for a minute they didn't know where they were. They were also very stiff from sleeping in such an awkward position and Harry had a bit if a headache.

'Wakey, wakey, sleepy heads,' George said quietly and soon they were staring up at him, obviously not sure what to do next.

He looked at them with a puzzled expression and then asked, 'You don't live around, here do you?'

PC and Harry looked at each other and then Harry started to explain while rubbing his head.

'No George, we are from the Channel Islands and are making our way home from Taunton. We left Chard this morning and are on our way to Weymouth to get the ferry to Guernsey. PC is from Guernsey and I am from Jersey.

A puzzled look came over Georges' face as he tried to take in what he had heard.

'Where are the Channel Islands?' George asked after giving up on his cogitation.

The boys looked at each other and Harry nodded to PC to explain.

'They are in the Bay of St Malo, just across the Channel, almost as far as France.' PC said, just a little bit more slowly than he normally spoke, as if talking to someone younger. 'They were occupied by the Germans in the war, so goodness knows what they'll be like when we get home.'

George looked at them wide eyed. 'Guess you won't be walking all the way home then.'

'No, that's why we are going to Weymouth to get the ferry,' Harry added, a little exasperated. Thankfully his headache was starting to pass.

'I've never been out of Axminster,' George replied, as if to explain his ignorance about the boy's home. 'Sounds nice though,' he added, as if to lighten the moment. 'I hope all will be well when you get there.'

'So, I guess you could do with a bed for the night,' he offered with a smile.

'That would be nice,' PC said with a big smile on his face.

'Well I can't offer you a guest bedroom lads, but there are staff quarters that are empty as we are a bit short staffed. Would you be happy to sleep down in the basement?'

Harry and PC both nodded appreciatively, and George ushered them around to a staff entrance and showed them into a very basic room not far from the kitchen with a couple of wooden cots with blankets laid out on them.

'Can we help in any way?' PC offered as a thank you for his hospitality.

'Well I think Chef may need some help preparing the vegetables if you are happy to do that.' George suggested and then popped out to see what needed doing. He was back within 5 minutes with a pair of aprons for the boys.

'Here you go, put these on and then head along the corridor to the kitchen and Chef will tell you what to do. While you are doing that, I'll just sort out your room to make it bit more comfortable for you.'

The boys put on their aprons and headed down to the kitchen where they were met by a scene that appeared to them like a vision of hell. The heat was intense, flames seemed to erupt from ovens and pans and around half a dozen men in various garbs resembling cooks and chefs fussed around in a haze of smoke, preparing food for the diners in the restaurant. In the centre of it all was a large, red faced man, with a tall chef's hat on who was controlling the madness like a conductor controls an orchestra.

He beckoned the boys over and in what seemed like an impossibly deep voice spoke to the boys.

'My name is Chef, nothing more, nothing less. If I hear you call me anything else you will feel the toe of my boot on your backsides, do you hear me?'

The boys nodded dumb founded by the enormous man standing over them.

'Now, go over to that corner of my kitchen and start peeling potatoes. The sack is under the sink and there is a basket for the peelings. Put the peeled potatoes in that pan of water after rinsing each one on the sink. Do you understand?'

The boys nodded again and stood there in shock.

'WELL WHAT ARE YOU WAITING FOR!!' Chef shouted and the boys sped off to their work.

He went back to his bench and as he did he caught the eye of one of his team and gave him a big wink. The assistant chef shook his head smiling and followed the boys to make sure they knew what they were doing.

The assistant chef stood behind the boys and showed them how to peel a potato using a gadget they had never seen before and quietly whispered in their ears. 'Don't worry, his bark is worse than his bite. If you get stuck give me a shout, my name is Jim by the way.' He smiled and left them to it.

With their potato peelers in hand the boys got to work and started attacking the sack of potatoes. It seemed like a never-ending job though because as soon as they had filled the pan someone came and emptied it and they had to start all over again. They couldn't believe how many potatoes were being eaten in the restaurant. When they did steal a look to see what was happening behind them, they could see the potatoes being boiled, roasted, mashed and sliced by different assistant chefs as each meal was prepared.

The boy's hands were getting red and cold as the continuous peeling and rinsing seemed to go on forever. Finally, Chef announced that this was the last order and told everyone involved in food preparation to stop what they were doing as the last meals were plated up.

The boys breathed a sigh of relief as Jim handed them a towel to dry their hands. He suggested they go over to the largest of the ranges and warm their hands. 'But don't get too close or you'll get chilblains,' he added.

The boys didn't know what chilblains were but were suitably scared to make sure they stood back from the range a little as the warmth gradually came back to their aching hands.

Two enormous hands landed on their shoulders as Chef came up behind them. Both boys winced.

'Well done boys. I have to say I didn't think you would keep up, but you did a great job.' The boys relaxed as they noticed his deep voice was now full of warmth.

He continued, 'I've laid out a bit of supper for you and a mug of hot milk to see you off to bed. You can take it with you to your room if you like.'

'Thanks Chef.' The boys echoed with a pair of big smiles. They went over to the work top and grabbed a plate each with a mug of steaming milk and headed along the corridor to their little room in the staff quarters.

By now it was quite dark and the small window high up the wall was black against the grey walls of the room. George had left them a lone candle which burned on a small table that had been set up for them. Their gear and the precious football were stowed at the bottom of the two beds and two single mattresses had been added and the beds properly made ready for them. They put the mugs on the table and tucked into their sandwiches.

Both of the lads were tired and after their sandwiches and a lot of talk about their kitchen experience and how scary Chef was, they soon had their shoes off and were snuggling under their blankets each cupping their hot milk in their hands and enjoying the feel of the warm liquid working its way down to their bellies.

Half an hour later George popped his head around the door to say goodnight, but he was too late. Both were sound asleep PC still with his mug his hands. George tiptoed over and took the mug gently from PC's hands and picked up the other mug and plates then blew the candle out and gently shut the door.

Chapter Six

The boys woke bright and early to the sound of pans crashing and Chef shouting at his breakfast team. There was also the delicious smell of bacon and eggs wafting under the closed door. Light was streaming through the small window and both boys could see blue sky.

'What do we do now?' Harry asked and PC responded with a stretch and a smile.

'I don't know but I could stay here a while longer.' PC replied.

'Well I need the loo for a start.' Harry announced. 'Come on, let's get ourselves ready for the day then I guess we need to head further south. How's your leg today by the way?'

'Feel's good thanks, hadn't even thought about it,' PC replied.

The boys put their shoes back on and headed out into the passageway. They got a glimpse of the kitchen and the organised chaos within and luckily, they saw Jim rushing about and waved him over. 'Where is the loo?' PC whispered and Jim just pointed to the far end of the passage and mouthed. 'On the right.'

The boys headed down as directed and found themselves in a pretty basic washroom. They took turns each to go to the toilet and took the opportunity to have a basic wash. Feeling refreshed they headed back to their room and while they were straightening their beds there was a knock on the door and George poked his head around. 'Fancy something to eat boys. We've got a couple of breakfasts going spare.'

'Yes please,' they responded together and followed George down to the kitchen where a cup of tea and a plate of bacon and eggs with fried tomatoes and some toast was waiting for both of them. The Chef paused and gave them a glower which turned into a slight smile before bellowing out more orders to his team as the bacon sizzled and the eggs splattered.

The boys tucked into the food, conscious that it might be a while before they ate again. Nothing was left.

George came to meet them and to see if they were OK.

'What you up to today then boys?' George asked.

'Well I think we are going to try and get down to the South Coast today.' PC suggested, looking at Harry.

'Yep,' Harry agreed. 'Not sure which way to go mind but I don't think we can be far away now.'

'Chef?' George called out. Chef dropped a spatula he was wielding quite dramatically and wiping his hands on a cloth tied to his waist, came over to join George and the boys.

George explained that the boys were trying to get home and needed to get down to the south coast and asked if Chef had ever been that way.

'When I came out of the army after coming back to England from Germany I actually came home from the south coast and it isn't that far. You need to take the Lyme road out of town and then take the main road down to Charmouth. I reckon it isn't much more than 5 miles so it shouldn't take that long.' Once you get there you turn left and head towards Weymouth.'

The boys looked at each other, genuinely excited that their goal was getting so close.

'Thank you so much for our breakfast and all your hospitality,' Harry offered to both George and Chef. PC nodded in agreement and offered his hand to Chef who promptly shook it, almost completely enclosing PC's hand in his own giant paw.

He then shook Harry's hand too and George joined in shaking the boy's hands in turn.

'Right, best crack on,' Chef announced, and he headed back to his work. 'Before you go though, take one of these each to see you on your way.' He turned and threw an apple to each of the boys and with a beaming smile they hadn't seen before and shouted 'Good Luck.' All his team joined in and applauded the boys as George took them out of the kitchen to get their gear. He then led them upstairs and out into the morning air.

'This might come in handy,' he said producing an old guide map to the south west which he told them would show them the way. He explained how it was given to him before the war and how it had been his prize possession growing up when he dreamed of visiting other places in the South West. Now he hoped it would guide them back home.

The boys were quite moved and PC asked George if he would sign their football which he duly did using a fountain pen he pulled out of his waistcoat pocket.

He took them out into the road and explained which road was the Lyme Road.

Harry on the spur of the moment took the ball from PC and dropped it on the road.

'You any good at football George?' Harry asked.

'I've played a bit.' George replied with a sly smile.

'Go on then, you take the kickoff and send us on our way.'

'OK,' George replied taking a couple of steps back and then taking a short run up he belted the ball as hard as he could towards the Lyme road.

‘Thanks George,’ PC yelled and with that they were off like mad things chasing the ball and kicking it down the road until George and the George Hotel were out of sight.

The boys spent some time kicking the ball along the Lyme Road then PC stopped for a rest and asked Harry to get out the map which he duly did.

‘This is a bit boring just following the road,’ PC suggested. ‘Why don’t we head across the fields and have a bit more of an adventure?’

‘Sounds like more fun than following the road,’ Harry replied and as soon as they got to the next gate, they climbed over it and headed off across the fields. They soon happened across a small brook and decided to follow it towards some woods they had seen in the general direction they were going. After a mixture of walking and climbing along the edge of the brook they decided to take a break. They both drank brook water in cupped hands and tucked into the apple that George had given them. The edges of the brook on both sides were lined with trees and they rested in the shade the trees provided, eventually closing their eyes and enjoying a nap in the warmth of that bright sunny late summer day.

Butterflies and various insects that liked the water buzzed around them creating a mystical scene where you could imagine fairies were hidden around every corner. A beautiful Kingfisher provided a flash of blue as it dived into the brook in search of the many small fish that teemed in the shallows while the gentle sound of the running water helped ease them to sleep.

The snap of a twig woke the boys with a start, and they were instantly alert wondering what had made the noise that had disturbed their slumber.

PC saw it first and nudged Harry pointing with his eyes as to where he should look.

Not twenty yards from them a young deer was drinking from the brook, seemingly oblivious to their presence. As they watched a second deer joined the first and soon what seemed like a dozen or more of the animals were making their way down to the side of the brook to take advantage of the cool water.

Suddenly one of the deer heard something and raised its head with a start. With a snort it turned and leaped away into the trees followed by all the others. The boys looked over to where the deer had looked and out of the forest appeared a fox. The beautiful creature made its way to the brook just like the deer and took a long drink. Harry moved slightly to get a better look and the fox was instantly aware of their presence and ran back into the forest leaving them alone again in the small clearing.

'Never seen a fox before,' PC whispered, still in the magic of the scene they had just witnessed.

'Nor me, haven't seen a deer before either. It looked just like Bambi,' replied Harry, recalling a book he had seen when he was much younger.

'Guess, we'd better get going,' PC replied conscious that he had no idea how long they had been asleep. The sun still seemed quite high, so he reckoned it hadn't been long.

They gathered themselves together with their bits and pieces, threw their apple cores into the brook, took one last drink and started off in the same direction as they were going before. Along the way they both made small twig boats and raced them along the brook. Their progress was very slow, but they were going in the right direction.

Soon they came out of the trees and spotted a truck over to their right driving along a road. They decided to get back to the road to make sure they didn't get lost.

As luck would have it, they rejoined the road just where it met the Charmouth road where they could see the white sign pointing the way to Charmouth. They had 4 miles to go.

'4 miles,' complained Harry.

'That's nothing, we'll be there in no time and then we can see the sea. And you know what that means.' PC smiled brightly.

'Yep, we are on our way home,' said Harry suddenly full of enthusiasm. 'Come on, I'll race you.'

With that they made off in the direction of Charmouth, the ball being enthusiastically kicked all the way.

On the way they passed the outskirts of Raymond's Hill but most of the rest of the way they saw nothing but farmland. They picked blackberries on the way and ducked inside field gates the few times a car or truck came past. They saw the occasional tractor at work and several fields of sheep and cows. The boys remarked about the black and white cows which sparked a debate as to whether Jersey or Guernsey cows were better but as neither had ever seen both types of cow together they couldn't really argue too much but both agreed the milk they remembered from home was much better than the milk they had drunk in England.

One group of cows was right by the road, watching them go by. Harry made a mooing sound and one of the cows mooed back which started a fun game as they both tried to enter into a "conversation" with the herd. One of the cows got quite agitated by this and started pushing at the gate which encouraged the boys to race off just in case it managed to break the gate down and charge at them.

The scenery was becoming more spectacular all the time as they started to head downhill towards the coast. They could see glimpses of the sea in the distance and bits of spectacular cliffs at the end of rolling hills. Soon they were on the outskirts of

Charmouth heading down through the small town and past a variety of small shops before suddenly, they saw signs for the beach and there in all its glory was the English Channel.

They made their way through the dragons teeth defences at the top of the beach, a stark reminder that the war was only just over, and headed across a beach mainly consisting of grey pebbles and almost as if it was a ceremony, touched the water as it gently lapped along the shore. They looked at each other and smiled. It felt like a connection, it felt like they were nearly home.

As they looked about, they could see several people moving along the beach seemingly looking for something. Off to their left the cliffs rose high into the sky and they could see more people walking around, heads down and from time to time bending down and rooting around in the pebbles.

Curious they headed off towards the nearest person to get a better look at what they were doing. The lady concerned eyed them a little suspiciously as they approached. She had a bonnet over her head, a dark jacket and a long thick dress that reached down to her ankles. She carried a wicker basket which seemed to hold several rocks and they noticed she had a small hammer tucked into the leather belt which held her skirt up.

'This is my spot,' she growled at the boys without straightening up from the bent position she was in as she examined the beach in front of her.

'What are you looking for?' PC ventured bravely.

'Ammonites,' was the terse reply.

'What's an ammonite?' Harry asked, joining in the conversation.

'This your first time here boy?' The woman looked at Harry with sharp eyes and the boys realised at this point that the woman was quite old, her skin bronzed and wrinkled from too much exposure to the sun.

'Yes,' Harry replied nervously. 'We are just passing through on our way to Weymouth.'

'You've got a long way to go,' the woman replied but she seemed to soften to the boys and beckoned them closer.

She took a grey rock out of her bag and showed the boys what she was collecting. There in the broken face of the pebble was a shiny brown coil of what she explained was an ancient sea creature called an ammonite. The fossil was 200 million years old she told the boys who stood open mouthed at this amazing revelation. They couldn't believe you could just find something as amazing as that on the beach.

'You can find other ancient creatures here too, but these are the most numerous,' she explained. 'I have been collecting them all my life and sell them to the shops in the town here and in Lyme Regis.'

'Have you ever found a dinosaur?' PC asked remembering the magazine story he had read a long time ago.

The woman smiled, 'I have found dinosaur bones, but never a whole dinosaur.'

Inspired by the amazing bounty to be found on the beach PC asked if they could try and find a dinosaur or an ammonite.

'Of course,' she replied. 'Have a wander over there. I don't have a spare hammer, but you can use another rock to crack the stones. See if you can find some with bits of the ammonite sticking out. They can be the best.'

The excited boys headed off to where she had pointed and started turning pebbles in search of ammonite bearing pebbles. They put the ball and their bags down and using that as a base pushed out in a wide circle scrabbling around sometimes on their hands and knees and other times bent over just like the woman. Soon their backs were aching, but PC was lucky and found an ammonite on the surface of a pebble. It was badly worn but gave them hope.

Harry found a large pebble with a tiny hole in it and carefully cracked the stone with another stone. After a couple of hits, it cracked right across where the little hole was and what it revealed made their jaws drop. The stone was simply full of ammonites all lying together at different angles, both of the exposed sides were covered in ammonites, so they had two beautiful examples of the creatures.

Excitedly they ran across to the old woman and showed them their find.

'I don't believe it,' she said, visibly amazed. 'Talk about beginner's luck.'

'Is that worth anything?' Harry asked.

'Oh yes,' she replied. 'The shopkeepers will pay you handsomely for those beauties. But you need to know how to haggle with them, do you want me to help you?'

'Yes please,' Harry replied,

The woman straightened her back with a bit of a groan and looked around, taking in the angle of the sun to try and work out what time it was.

'I tell you what, let's keep looking for another hour then we will pop into town and see what we can get for your ammonites and any others you might find,'

'OK,' Harry replied excitedly, and the boys hurried back to their spot and continued the hunt.

After an hour the boys had little more to show for their efforts. PC had a nice single ammonite which he had found but nothing compared to Harry's group of ammonites.

The woman, whose name turned out to be Rita, had quite a few nice examples of ammonites in her basket. She called out to them and the boys gathered up their bits and pieces and together they headed back up the beach towards town.

They stopped outside a small shop with a sign over the window which simply said Fossil Shop. In the corner of the window was a small sign saying fossils bought for cash. They all trooped in and Rita headed across to the counter and started speaking to the owner who she obviously knew very well.

'What have you got for me today Rita?' the shop owner asked. 'You found a few younger fossils today I see,' he added, looking at the boys over the rim of his glasses with a big smile.

'These young lads have never been on the beach before and found the best fossil I have seen in many a long day,' Rita told the shopkeeper.

'Let's have a look then.'

Rita emptied the contents of her basket on the counter and sorted them out so he could see the various ammonites they had found. He took out an eye piece, pushing his glasses on to his forehead and looked at each ammonite in detail, making appreciative grunts and noises in the process. While this was happening, the boys took the opportunity to look around the shop and admire the many fossils on display. It was obvious that some extra work was done after the fossils were found as many of the ammonites for sale seemed more prominent on their stones than the one's they had found. Some almost seemed to glow so maybe a polish or lacquer had been applied to the creature to help make it stand out.

‘This is amazing,’ the boys heard the shopkeeper say as he eventually came to Harry’s stone.

‘What are you prepared to give us for that one then?’ Rita asked.

‘How about 12 shillings,’ the man suggested.

Harry almost choked coughing. He was amazed at the thought of his stone being worth that amount of money. However, Rita seemed less than impressed and suggested that a shop in Lyme she knew would offer her double that.

Haggling continued for a while until a Guinea was settled on for Harry’s stone and sixpence for each of the other stones, PC’s included.

Money changed hands and the group headed out of the shop. They headed over to the Wander Inn Cafe and Rita ordered cream cakes and tea all round. As they were waiting to be served, she counted out 21 shillings and 6 pence and gave the money to the boys.

‘Well, what are you going to do with your money boys?’

‘Not sure,’ Harry replied. ‘We’ll need somewhere to stay the night so I guess we could look for somewhere around here now it is getting a bit late. We also have some money saved to pay for our tickets home’

PC whispered in Harry’s ear. ‘Oh yes, and we’ll pay for these too, he announced as the tea and cakes appeared.

‘Well that is very kind. Where are you from?’ Rita asked.

While they drank and ate their cakes the boys took it in turn to tell their story and how they were heading to Weymouth to catch a ferry home to the Channel Islands. Rita listened attentively as the story was told and, in the end, felt sorry for the boys, especially Harry who had lost his father at Dunkirk.

Eventually the lovely china teapot ran dry and the last crumb and drop of cream had been licked from their plates.

'Rita, do you know of anywhere we can stay?' PC finally asked.

Rita thought for a moment. 'Well I have a friend who runs a small Hotel, we can ask her.'

'That would be great,' Harry replied. With that Harry very bravely asked for the bill and paid over the shilling and 9 pence.

Rita smiled as she got up from the table with a 'Thank you, young sir.' She then led them out of the tea shop and took them to a lovely looking hotel, coincidentally called the George Inn. Rita knocked on the door and spoke to a lovely lady called Edith who beckoned them all in.

Edith ushered the boys into the living room and gave them each a drink of lemonade then left them while she spoke to Rita.

'Did you see the name over the door?' PC asked Harry.

'The George Inn.' Harry replied with a smile. 'That's a coincidence.'

'I know,' PC replied. 'What a day, we start off at the George Hotel, spent sometime in the woods, saw some amazing animals, kicked the football all the way to Charmouth, found some amazing fossils and earned a load of money, met an amazing lady who has the same name as my Mum and ended up in the George Inn.'

Harry sat back in his chair and smiled, drinking his lemonade. 'It was brilliant.'

With that the owner of the hotel and Rita came back in.

'This is Edith, a good friend, who owns this lovely Hotel with her husband. I explained all about you and where you are going and she is happy for you to spend the night here for a shilling each. That includes breakfast and the use of the bathroom upstairs.'

'A shilling blurted out Harry, that seems a lot.'

Rita looked at him with a furrowed brow. 'I'll have you know young man that is very cheap and a special price just for you. How many hotels have you stayed in recently?'

Harry looked very sheepish. 'None, sorry,' he whispered.

Edith was smiling away behind the boys as they looked at each other furtively.

'No offence taken boys,' Edith said. 'Come on. I'll show you your room.'

They went to leave the room and leave Rita behind. As they did PC stopped and looked back at Rita.

'Will we see you tomorrow?' He asked.

'Not likely,' Rita replied. 'I'll be down on the beach as soon as I can.'

'Thank you for all your help Rita, it has been really kind of you.' With that he went across and gave Rita a big hug. Harry followed and did the same.

PC offered out his football. 'Will you sign my football for me please?'

'Of course.' Rita replied.

Without having to be asked, Edith fetched a pen from the reception desk in the hall and offered it to Rita who promptly signed the ball, noticing all the other signatures that people had left. PC then asked Edith to sign the ball too which she did in turn.

With that the boys took their things and followed Edith up the stairs and Rita gave them a wave from the bottom of the stairs.

After she had settled them in Edith came down and met Rita again in the lounge.

She got a bottle of whiskey out of the cupboard and poured out two glasses.

'Cheers.' Edith offered, clinking glasses with Rita.

'Look after them Edith please. They are two special young lads who have been through a lot of trauma in their young lives.'

'I will,' Edith replied with a smile. 'I can see they mean a lot to you.'

'You know I lost my son in the war don't you,' Rita replied. 'The world needs young men like these if it is going to rebuild after the horror of the last 5 years. If you can set them on the right road after breakfast tomorrow, I would really appreciate it.'

'Don't worry Rita, they'll be safe here, and I'll make sure they are well fed before they head off towards home.'

'Thank you, Edith, and if you need any money from me to help, just let me know. The fossils have been good to me lately.'

‘There’ll be no need for that Rita, business is picking up now the war is over. The Americans were good to us too while they were here, we’ll miss them.’

‘That we will,’ smiled Rita. ‘There will be quite a few of my ammonites making their way across the Atlantic over the next few months.’

‘How about a toast,’ Edith suggested. ‘To PC and Harry and to sunny days.’

They both smiled, clinked glasses again and downed their drinks.’

‘Time for one more Edith offered.’

‘Why not,’ Rita replied with a laugh.

*****

Upstairs PC and Harry had taken turns in the bathroom and were settling down on their beds reading a couple of comics Edith had given them. Their room was lovely with an aspidistra in a large jardiniere which stood in front of the window. The view from the window looked out on to the main street through Charmouth which was still busy with people walking down to the beach to enjoy the evening air. The wallpaper in the room was mainly pink with a rose design and the two single beds were spotlessly clean with patchwork quilts on the top of each. A small table separated them and on that stood a small vase with a posy of flowers in it. Alongside stood a single candle, which Edith had lit for them.

They could hear the women chatting and laughing downstairs, but Edith had promised them something to eat before they went to bed so they waited eagerly, tummies rumbling as they hadn’t eaten much that day.

After half an hour it went quiet downstairs and before long there was a knock on the door and PC leapt up to open it.

Edith came in with a tray on which were a couple of rounds of beef sandwiches and two steaming cups of hot chocolate.

'Here you go lads, Rita asked me to look after you and that's exactly what I intend to do. Is this OK for you?'

'That's super,' Harry said with real enthusiasm. He grabbed a sandwich and then suddenly felt a pang of guilt. 'Sorry about before, I had no idea what staying in a hotel cost and have only ever had a few pennies in my pocket before.'

Edith put her hand on his shoulder. 'That's OK son,' she said with feeling. 'I understand, but you can trust me. I have promised Rita I will look after you and I will.'

'Thank you,' the boys said in unison and with meaning.

'I'll see you in the morning, I'll give you a knock about 8 am, but if you need anything just ring that bell,' she said, pointing to a lever by the door.

With that she turned and left the boys to enjoy their supper and hot chocolate.

'I'd never had hot chocolate before this trip,' PC said after savouring the steaming drink.

Harry smiled. 'It's great. When I have my own place, I am going to drink hot chocolate every day.'

The boys laughed and enjoyed their feast before settling down to sleep.

What a day it had been.

Chapter Seven

Two days after the boys left Axminster, the peace of the small town was shattered as two US Army jeeps rushed into town and screeched to a halt near the church. Karl and Christine were in one and Catherine and new recruit to the search, Derek, from New Jersey was in the other.

The four Americans jumped out of the jeep and fanned out around the centre of the town, knocking on doors and asking residents if they had seen the two boys. Catherine was talking to one shopkeeper who suggested talking to the staff at the George Hotel as he seemed to recall seeing a couple of young lads working there. Catherine called Christine over and together they went over to the Hotel where Karl was already talking to a young lad under the archway.

As they approached the member of staff ran off into the Hotel and Karl explained that he was getting someone who may know the boys.

After a couple of minutes George appeared and asked what was happening.

Sister Christine explained that they were looking for two boys who had disappeared from Musgrove Park Hospital in Taunton and that they were worried about their health. George was a bit nervous about saying anything which might cause trouble for PC and Harry but was also worried for the two lads as they may be causing themselves harm by not convalescing as they should.

He considered denying all knowledge for a moment but when he saw the real concern on the faces of the two nurses and thought about the effort they were putting into finding the boys he quickly realised that it was in their best interest to be found and helped back to full health.

'Yes, they were here,' he finally admitted.

Both nurses gasped with relief to know they were finally on the right trail.

George explained to the friends how the boys had arrived and all that happened while they had stayed at the George. He also mentioned what they had told him that they had come from Chard and how Chef had suggested they take the Lyme Road and head for Charmouth before heading east towards Weymouth.

Derek had appeared by now and added that someone had seen the boys kicking a ball down the Lyme road. This confirmed that they had done as Chef suggested but of course that was two days ago and they could have walked to Weymouth by now.

They all looked at Sister Christine as to what to do next.

She thought for a moment. Looking at her watch she came to a decision.

'Right, we have no clue where they might be now and we won't be able to extend the search for a couple of days so let's head back to Chard and see if we can find where they stayed and if we can get any more clues as to how they are and what their plans might be.'

'OK boss, saddle up everybody,' Karl announced, waving a finger in the air in a circular motion like a cowboy, and soon they were back in the jeeps and heading back north to Chard.

Chapter Eight

The boys woke early after their night at the George Inn and nattered in bed until Edith knocked on the door at 8am sharp.

'Wakey, wakey, rise and shine,' Edith sang as she walked into the room carrying a tray with bowls of hot porridge and two tall glasses of milk.

The boys sat themselves up in bed and she handed each a bowl, set on a plate, together with a spoon and placed the two glasses of milk on the small table.

'You couldn't get better service in a coffee shop,' she added with a smile.

'Thank you so much,' Harry said with a big grin while PC, who already had a mouth full of porridge simply nodded in agreement.

Edith left them to it and the boys tucked into their breakfast. When they were finished, they took turns to visit the bathroom and freshen up before getting properly dressed and preparing themselves for the day ahead. They put on fresh underwear and cleanish shirts and once their small bags were packed and the football was tucked safely under PC's arm they sat on their beds and discussed what to do next.

'This is such a nice place I hope I get to come here again,' PC mused.

Harry agreed and produced the map George had given them from his pocket.

He laid it out on the bed, and they poured over it for a while, seeing how far they had come and how many miles they still had to go until they reached Weymouth.

‘It looks like we need to head towards Abbotsbury which is on the way to Weymouth.’ Harry said, pointing at the map and the route. They looked up the map scale and using their fingers worked out in a rather rudimentary fashion that it was around 15 or 16 miles to Abbotsbury, which given the rolling hills they had seen on the way into Charmouth, would probably take them most of the day.

‘Yep, but that will break the back of the journey as it’s not as far to go from Abbotsbury to Weymouth.’ PC replied, describing the distance left as a gap between his thumb and his index finger.

‘I wonder what time it is now?’ PC asked, knowing Harry didn’t know the answer.

‘Guess we’ll find out if we go downstairs and get started.’ Harry replied with a smile.

PC lay back on his bed. ‘But this is so comfortable, who knows where we will be sleeping tonight.’

Harry stood up and held out his hand to give PC a pull off the bed. ‘Come on mate, best foot forward and all that. The sooner we get going the sooner we get home.’

PC allowed himself to be pulled off the bed and picked his bag up and with the football tucked under his arm followed Harry out of their cosy hotel room and down the stairs into the reception area. In the lounge they spotted Edith having a cup of tea and reading a paper.

She looked up. ‘You lads on your way now?’

Harry reached into his pocket and pulled out a Florin. ‘Thank you so much for looking after us Edith,’ he hesitated a little before using her first name. ‘Here’s a florin for the room.’

Edith put her paper down and got up, giving each of the boys a hug in turn.

'You can put your money away Harry, save it for your journey. It may come in useful before you get home. Wait there a minute, I've got something for you.' With that she disappeared through the back of reception, soon coming back with a brown paper bag which she handed over to Harry.

'Here you go boys. Some sandwiches, a bit of cheese and an apple each. That should keep you going for the day. Are you off towards Abbotsbury?' she asked.

'Thank you so much,' PC said peeking into the bag which Harry had opened. 'I think we can make Abbotsbury today but going straight to Weymouth would be a bit too far in one day.'

'I think that's a good choice,' Edith offered. 'Whatever you do don't go along the beach to Abbotsbury as the tide can be a bit iffy and occasionally they have cliff falls, but when you get there look out for the swannery, it is a beautiful sight to behold.'

'Thanks for the advice,' Harry replied and gave Edith a hug of thanks. 'Right, time to go,' he said, wiping a tear from his eye. With that the boys headed to the front door and down the hill from the hotel. Stopping briefly outside the gate to wave to Edith who was standing in the doorway, waving a handkerchief to the boys as they walked away.

'We'll be back,' shouted PC as they disappeared from sight.

Edith wiped a tear from her eye and went back inside the George Inn, '*I hope so,*' she thought. '*I hope so.*'

The boys walked down the hill as far as the top of the beach and looked along the coast in the direction they needed to travel. Waves broke on the shore and a haze of moisture filled the air adding a supernatural look to the figures who walked the beach or stooped looking for fossils. They crossed a small wooden bridge at the mouth of the River Char and followed the path east towards the cliffs which rolled away in the direction they had to walk.

The path was quite steep in places as they walked amongst the dune type scrub land, thick with mixed grasses and plants amongst patches of sand. Further off to their left were fields, some of which were full of cattle. As they gained height, they looked back towards Charmouth and got a last look, wistfully, at the small town where the two kind ladies lived that had helped them so much. Eventually they topped the hill and Charmouth was gone and several miles of cliff path lay ahead. For the first time PC was able to drop the ball without risk of it rolling back down the way they had come and off they went, excited about the next leg of their journey.

Ahead they could see a particularly high piece of cliff and they knew Abbotsbury was on the other side of that hill.

Chapter Nine

After a stiff walk which caused PC the odd twinge in his leg, the boys could finally see Abbotsbury. They could also hear the swannery and surmised it must be feeding time.

They had left the cliff path at West Bay and followed the road which ran alongside the cliff tops until they had seen their destination. They had diverted off the road on to a path to try and get to the swannery to see why it was so special. It ended up being a rather circuitous route, passing a small chapel as they went. They ended up making their way down a path towards the swannery which bypassed the town altogether.

The sight of hundreds and hundreds of swans was amazing. They headed into the swannery and were soon walking amongst them. A man was feeding the birds down by the side of Fleet lagoon. It looked as if the swans in front of him were locked together to make a huge white raft. The man saw the boys and asked them if they wanted to help him feed the swans and soon the three of them were throwing out wheat grains to the huge bevy of swans.

Philip introduced himself to the boys as the swanherd for the Abbotsbury swannery and explained there had been a swannery there for hundreds of years. He showed them around the site and then asked what had brought them to the swannery. The boys explained that they had come from Charmouth and the owner of the George Inn had suggested they look out for the swannery on their journey to Weymouth.

The boys had been walking for around 7 hours or so and had eaten their sandwiches on the way and were already feeling hungry and wondering about their next meal.

'Do you know if there is anywhere around here, where we can get some food and stay the night?' Harry asked the swanherd.

Philip rubbed his chin in thought.

‘One of the farms on the edge of town has a couple of letting rooms, maybe they would take you in?’ Philip suggested pointing back up towards the town.

‘You’re a bit young to be travelling by yourselves, though aren’t you?’ He added with a furrowed brow.

‘We are trying to get home sir,’ PC blurted out. ‘We live in the Channel Islands and need to get a ferry from Weymouth to get ourselves home.’

‘Were you evacuated here then?’ Philip asked curious to know how they had ended up in Abbotsbury.

‘We were in Taunton,’ Harry explained, ‘and we missed our coach so decided to make our own way home.’

‘You’ve done well to get this far.’ Philip stated with a smile.

‘You don’t have far to go now. Come on I’ll take you up to the farm.’

Soon they had walked up into the town of Abbotsbury and Philip was knocking on the door of a pretty farmhouse with roses creeping over the front door. As they waited the boys noted the paint was peeling off the window frame, the garden was a bit of a mess and there were weeds on the path. As they were looking around the door opened, and an old man appeared. He looked quite fragile and walked with a stick.

‘What have we here Philip?’ the old man asked.

‘These two lads are looking for a bed for the night and something to eat, can you help?’

‘I think we can help. Leanne,’ he called over his shoulder. With that a young girl in her early 20’s came smiling to the door.

'What's up Granddad?'

'Have we got room for these two nippers?' He asked.

'I reckon we can manage that. I guess you two might be looking for something to eat too.'

'Yes please.' PC replied.

'What about you Philip?' Leanne offered with a beautiful smile aimed at the handsome swanherd.

'That would be lovely,' Philip replied eagerly. 'I need to go back and finish off around the swannery, what time shall I come back?'

'How about 5.30?' Leanne suggested.

'That's perfect thank you. See you later.' Philip smiled back and then headed off to the swannery as Leanne and her Granddad ushered the boys inside their small farmhouse.

Inside the boys were taken through to a small kitchen with a large aga, a large belfast sink and a wooden table with 6 chairs. A welsh dresser filled the wall opposite the aga and that was covered with plates, cups and other assorted china. Leanne put a large copper kettle on the aga to make tea while her Granddad took a seat at the table and asked the boys to join him. Soon they were all sitting down drinking tea and Granddad asked the boys to tell him their story.

PC and Harry told them how they had made their way from Taunton to Abbotsbury, skipping the bit about sneaking away from the hospital, and what they planned to do next.

Granddad accepted their story without question and suggested the best way for them to get to Weymouth would be to walk along Chesil Beach as it runs straight to Portland which is next to Weymouth. Leanne agreed but expressed her concern that walking on the shingle wouldn't be easy, but the boys decided that was the way they would go.

'Right, we have a couple of hours before tea. Are you happy with liver, onions and mash with some gravy boys?' Leanne asked.

'Yes please,' the boys replied in unison.

'The only question is, how are you going to pay for your tea and for your stay?' Granddad asked looking serious.

'We have some money,' PC offered.

'We may need that for our tickets home,' Harry said quietly, nudging his friend.

Leanne looked at her Granddad. 'What about the garden Granddad, it needs a good weed.'

Granddad thought for a moment.

'That's a good idea Leanne. Get them to pick some fruit for pudding as well.'

'Would that be OK with you two? Leanne asked.

The boys both nodded thinking it was better than shoveling horse manure as they had done in Axminster.

Leanne smiled and took the boys out the back of the farmhouse to a small shed where a few tools were stored. Harry took a hoe and a bucket while PC picked up a spade and a bucket. Leanne then took them around the side of the house to the front garden and showed them which paths to weed.

'You've got about an hour so do as much as you can and then I'll bring a bowl out so you can pick some fruit. We have loganberries, raspberries, blackcurrants and strawberries ready to pick.'

'Yum,' Harry said with a smile as they started work.

Time flew as they worked. They managed to fill several buckets with weeds and tipped them around the back of the house on a spoil heap which Leanne had shown them earlier. Then she came out with a large bowl ready to pick the fruit for supper.

The three of them headed to a patch of ground behind the shed where Granddad had planted all his fruit. A loganberry bush grew up the wall at the back of the shed and there were beds where strawberry, blackcurrant and raspberry plants were full of fruit. In no time at all the bowl was full and the boys followed Leanne back into the house. The fruit was washed in a colander using a pump outside the back door and the boys were given the opportunity to clean themselves up before tea using the same pump. They took turns to go to the loo in a brick outhouse alongside the shed before Philip arrived for tea.

When they got back into the house the smell of frying liver and onions was amazing and the boys were almost drooling as they sat around the table waiting for Leanne to dish up the food.

During the meal the conversation centred around the boys and their journey and what they were expecting when they got home. Harry went quiet and PC took it upon himself to explain that Harry's dad had been killed in 1940 and he would be going back to hopefully live with his grandparents as his mum had died during the war.

Everyone went quiet for a while.

Leanne put her hand on Harry's arm. 'It will be alright Harry, you are young and you have your whole life ahead of you. I can tell having met you and by talking to you that you are strong, well beyond your years and you will have a great life.

You have so much to look forward to I am sure your Mum and Dad would want you to be happy so get home and enjoy what's coming. It will be fun, trust me!'

Harry smiled and everyone around the table nodded. 'Well said,' Philip said in agreement, echoing how everyone felt.

By then all the food has been eaten so Leanne cleared the dishes, with some help from Philip and then she took 5 bowls from the dresser and dished out the fruit. There was a small amount of precious sugar available and they all took a small spoonful of it and spread it over their fruit. It was delicious.

The conversation carried on until around 8pm when Philip announced he needed to get back to the swannery before it was completely dark. As he left, he shook the boy's hands and wished them well, hoping he would meet them again soon.

Leanne saw Philip out and then returned to show the boys to their room. While they were gardening, she had taken their bags and the football up to their room and prepared it for them with fresh bedding in the twin beds which virtually filled the small room. A single candle was all the light that was available and together with two cups of water it sat on a narrow table which separated the beds.

Leanne suggested the boys go to the toilet before it was properly dark and they agreed both taking turns to make the journey out to the toilet in the garden, washing their hands with water from the outdoor pump. As Harry came back in Granddad was sitting in the kitchen and called him over pulling out the seat next to his so Harry could sit down.

'Leanne knows what she is talking about,' he stated quietly. 'Her parents were killed in a bombing raid in 1940 while she was living here with me. They had sent her here to keep her safe and as it happened saved her life. She couldn't even attend their funeral to say goodbye and only recently came back from visiting London to see what remained of their house.'

Harry was quiet for a moment. 'I am so sorry to hear that. Is she alright?' he asked.

'She seems so on the outside, but I can't really get her to talk about it,' Granddad replied. 'Anyway, I just wanted you to know and to explain why when she spoke, it was from the heart.'

'Thanks Granddad,' Peter replied, getting up to go to bed. 'And thank you for all your kindness.'

'Don't thank me lad,' Granddad replied. 'I would have sent you two whippersnappers packing if it had been down to me. Leanne is the one to thank.'

He smiled and winked then waved Harry away.

Back in the room Harry told PC what Granddad had told him.

'There has been so much sadness everywhere we have been and yet people have been so nice.' Peter said while he got himself into bed.

'Something to remember when we grow up.' Harry replied pulling the cover up to his chin.

Soon the boys were sound asleep. It had been a busy day what with the walking, gardening and emotional turmoil they had experienced. Once again, they had found the right people to help them through another day.

*****

Next morning the boys were up bright and early. Breakfast was already on the go when they came downstairs. Jam made from their own fruit and toast from bread Leanne had made were already on the table. The toast was made by laying the bread on the hot plate on top of the aga so it was a little burnt in places but the taste of the jam and the rich butter led to no complaints from the boy who ate as much as they could to set them up for the day.

'What's the plan boys?' Granddad asked.

'I think we should press on as soon as we can sir,' PC replied. 'We still have a way to walk before we get to Weymouth.'

'Are you going to go along Chesil Beach then,' Leanne asked as she was pouring the inevitable cup of tea.

'I think so,' Harry said looking at PC. PC nodded in agreement. 'It sounds like it could be quite an adventure.'

'As soon as you are ready, I'll walk down with you to get you started. I might pop in to see Philip while I am down there and help him feed the swans,' she added looking at her Granddad.

'I reckon that's a good 12 miles walk and it's warm today, so you'd best take some water. Leanne can make you a sandwich to take with you too and some fruit.' Granddad offered.

Soon a brown paper bag full of cheese sandwiches had been prepared and an old water bottle which looked like it had been used in the war was filled to the brim. Then a small tin was found in a drawer and stuffed with fruit for them to take with them.

'There'll be nothing to forage for on the beach,' Leanne pointed out, 'so you'll need to crack on and when you have a drink, just sip it. When you get to the end of the beach cut across the narrow spit of land and you'll see Weymouth ahead of you. I reckon if you don't hang around you should get there by mid-afternoon.'

'Will you be alright?' Granddad asked, obviously concerned for the boys.

'We'll be fine sir,' PC replied, 'just the last part of our adventure. We could be home tomorrow,' he added with a smile.

'I hope so boys. Travel safe.'

Thank you, sir,' Harry offered. 'Will you sign PC's football before we leave?'

'Of course,' Granddad replied and soon he and Leanne had added their names to the battered ball.

Granddad's shook hands with Harry and PC and then waved them away before he got too emotional. Leanne led the boys out the front door and then the three of them walked down towards the coast. On the way they chatted about the swannery and Leanne explained she often helped Philip with the swans. The boys couldn't help noticing, that she really did look forward to spending time with the swanherd. Her smile and her enthusiasm to get to the swannery spoke volumes.

Harry looked at PC at one point and winked as Leanne spoke about how handsome Philip was.

Soon they were down by the swannery and Leanne led them around the Fleet lagoon on to the shingle which comprised Chesil beach. Together they walk up on to the top of the mound of pebbles.

The boys couldn't believe their eyes. Stretching out before them, as far as they could see, the marvel that is Chesil Beach lay before them.

'There's our way home,' Harry said, awed by the natural spectacle that confronted them. 'If we can follow this beach to the end we are almost in Weymouth and then all we have to do is work out how to get the boat home.'

PC stared for a long moment. Leanne broke the spell. 'Well boys, I have to love you and leave you. Be careful and if you are ever back in England don't forget to pop by.'

She gave them both a hug and turned back towards her home. She turned once and waved. With that the boys turned back towards their chosen way home.

'That's a lot of pebbles,' PC finally said, which was quite an understatement.

Harry laughed out loud and PC joined in.

'Come on,' Harry said. 'The sooner we start the sooner we will get home.'

With that the boys started their journey south towards Portland Bill and Weymouth. It was almost 10 am and the sun was starting to get warm as they began their long walk along Chesil Beach. It was soon apparent that walking on the pebbles wasn't easy and after a few attempts at kicking the ball ahead they chose to stumble along in silence except when the odd unusual pebble came to light or they passed a fisherman trying to catch his meal for the day. After an hour or so of walking they stopped to dip their feet in the water, rolling up their trousers and paddling out to their knees. It was so nice and cool they both wished they could stop and enjoy the beach for a bit longer, but after half an hours rest, they pushed on.

They seemed to be making good but slow progress as when they looked back, they couldn't see where they had started and by noon when the sun was at its highest they stopped again for another paddle. This time PC decided he would go for a proper swim and stripped down to his pants. Harry wasn't that comfortable in the water and decided to just paddle as he had done before.

PC waded bravely in, starting to feel the cold as soon as the water passed his knees. He kept shouting for Harry to join him but as he turned around to wave him in, he slipped and was instantly in deep water, he hadn't realised just how steep the beach was. He turned to swim back and started to struggle. He was a good swimmer but for some reason it seemed he couldn't get back to the beach.

'Help,' PC yelled as Harry watched from the shore. 'I can't get back', he puffed through the effort of swimming, spitting out water as he pushed harder to get back.

Harry didn't know what to do. He couldn't swim out and save him and there wasn't a soul in sight for miles around.

PC was in real trouble now, he was splashing and gurgling as he went under the water between efforts to swim.

'Help me Harry,' he managed. 'HELP ME!'

Harry looked around and had a brain wave. He grabbed the football and walked to the water's edge. By this time PC was about 30 yards out and really floundering.

Harry's heart was beating as he took aim and drop kicked the ball out towards his friend.

His aim was true, and the ball landed just a couple of feet from PC who immediately made a grab and hung on for dear life.

PC took a moment to regain his composure and then waved to Harry and shouted 'Thank you'.

After a few minutes rest and with the support of the ball he started to make his way slowly back towards the shore, kicking and using his spare arm to move himself forward. He finally touched the shingle around 100 yards further down the beach. Harry had shadowed him all the way, carrying their things and he helped pull PC back on to the beach as soon as he was close enough to reach.

The friends sat on the shingle for a while as PC dried out and finally stopped shaking. Probably the result of the cold and the shock.

'Thanks Harry,' PC finally said. 'That was a pretty good kick.'

'Well we've had a lot of practice,' Harry replied with a big smile. 'You would have done the same for me.' And with that he held out his hand and PC shook it.

'I would' PC replied looking his friend straight in the eyes.

'Guess that makes us blood brothers now you've saved my life,' PC added, as he started to get dressed. 'Like Red Indian warriors, fighting the cowboys'

He started to make Indian noises whooping and tapping his hand against his mouth, Harry joined in and soon they had both found seagull feathers and stuck them in their hair and were doing an Indian dance, going round in circles and whooping as loud as they could.

'You alright boys?' a fisherman asked as he walked past, and they nearly jumped out of their skins. He laughed his head off and continued walking. They sheepishly smiled at each other and picked up their gear before heading off towards the sun again and their goal, the town of Weymouth.

*****

It was nearly five in the afternoon before the friends could make out the end of the beach. They were absolutely starving now having finished all their food. Even the water bottle was empty. They were starting to appreciate why Bill had suggested not to walk Chesil Beach as their legs were aching from walking on the pebbles. They wished they had kept to the land where they might have had the opportunity to snack on blackberries or any fruit, they might have been able to scrump, like apples hanging over a hedge or a fence.

‘We need to get something to eat,’ PC stated, looking around as if he could find a sandwich amongst the stones.

Harry pulled PC’s arm and started to run as best they could across the pebbles towards the end of the beach.

‘We need to get off this beach before it gets dark.’

The boys made their way as quick as they could across the pebbles towards the end of Chesil Beach and the Isle of Portland. The sun was starting to get low in the West as the boys stumbled across some fisherman’s huts. Though their stomachs were rumbling they recognised they needed somewhere to spend the night. The temperature was already dropping after the heat of the day and the opportunity of snuggling up in a pile of nets seemed too good to miss.

‘We’ll get something at breakfast,’ PC said yawning as they tried to make themselves comfortable.

He wriggled around trying to get comfortable and then let out a yell.

‘What’s the matter,’ Harry asked concerned at the obvious pain his friend was in.

‘Something is stuck in my leg.’

Harry looked at his friend’s leg in the fading light and could see the glint of metal attached to a string. He gently pulled the string and PC let out a yelp.

He looked around at where his friend was lying and saw other bits of metal glinting in the light. ‘Fishhooks,’ he muttered to himself.

‘Don’t move PC, you’ve a fishhook in your leg.’

Harry jumped up and took a look around the Fisherman's Hut and in the dark managed to find a knife on a bench and used it to cut the line attached to the hook to free PC from his ties.

He helped PC get up carefully, making sure he didn't catch himself on the other hooks and then helped him out of the hut so they could sit on the beach.

'It hurts,' PC complained, tears glinting in the fading light. The sky was now full of deep reds and purples. At any other time, it would have been beautiful but now for the boys it heralded the dark and Harry wanted to find help for his friend.

As they sat Harry glimpsed some lights in the distance and shouted for help.

The lights made their way closer and soon materialised into a group of fishermen out to do some night fishing. 'What's up son,' one of them asked, bending down to look at the boys, his lamp illuminating their faces.

'My friend has a fishhook in his leg,' Harry muttered nervously.

'Let's have a look,' the Fisherman said, moving the light down to PC's leg.

There in the light they could all see the shaft of the hook sticking out of PC's calf. A small piece of line was left, tied on to the eye of the hook.

'Well you've got yourself caught good and proper,' the Fisherman said, smiling at the boys. 'The thing is with fishhooks is that you can't pull them out, they have a barb on the end, and they would rip your skin if you tried.'

'What we can do is cut the eye off and the push the hook so it will come out point first. It will hurt like mad though.

Otherwise we can take you to hospital and they can give you something for the pain while they take it out.'

The boys looked at each other. They feared that if they were taken to hospital they may be caught and taken back to Torquay rather make their way home as they planned.

'Take it out,' PC said bravely.

'OK,' the Fisherman said. 'Ray have you got your pliers and Ed, do you have your usual whiskey flask with you?'

Both the other fishermen nodded and reached into the bags they were carrying.

The Fisherman, whose name was Sam, took the whiskey and took a gulp before tipping some on the hook and wound. He then got the pliers and took the eye of the hook off with a quick snip. Then using the pliers, he gripped the exposed top of the hook and offered the whiskey flask to PC.

'Take a swig of this,' he urged without offering the chance for PC to decline.

PC took the flask. One of the fishermen moved behind PC and held his shoulders while the other grabbed his leg. Harry held PC's free hand.

'Make sure it's a big one,' Sam suggested.

PC took a sniff and then took a big gulp of the whiskey.

He winced with the shock as the liquid hit the back of his throat. At the same moment Sam push the shaft of the hook down until the point came out of PC's calf and then deftly grabbed the barb and pulled the hook out.

PC let out a scream and bucked but the Fishermen held him down. Harry yelped too as PC's fingernails bit into his hand, but the job was done.

Sam took the whiskey and poured a drop more on to the wound, took another swig himself and handed it back to his friend.

'Sorry Ed, not much left,' Sam said with a smile, wiping some sweat from his brow with the sleeve of his coat.

'Bloody kids,' Ed muttered as he shoved the half empty flask back into his bag.

Sam took a handkerchief from his pocket and tied it around PC's calf as a crude bandage and sat back to look at his handy work.

PC had stopped crying now and Harry was rubbing his hand where PC had squeezed it so tight.

'How are you feeling,' he asked PC.

'OK, my throat feels a bit sore though,'

The three laughed. 'You'll get used to the taste when you get older,' Ed said.

'Can I have a taste?' Harry asked.

'No!' was the gruff reply.

Sam laughed again.

'You boys have a home to go to?' Sam asked.

Harry looked at PC.

‘We were on our way home but got lost so thought we’d stop here for the night. We are on our way to Weymouth.’ Harry explained.

‘You don’t sound like you’re from around here,’ Sam suggested, becoming curious.

‘No, we are from the Channel Islands and will be on our way home soon,’ Harry added.

The fishermen looked at each other.

Ray, who was still sitting behind the boys, put his hands on their shoulders and squeezed them gently.

‘You lot had it tough over there, I hope all will be OK when you get home, are you hungry?’

The boys both nodded and soon the Fishermen were dipping into their bags and sharing out their sandwiches. The boys ate greedily and enjoyed a cup of tea from the flasks the men had with them.

‘Ever been night fishing?’ Sam asked the boys.

‘Never,’ Harry replied.

‘Well let’s show you how it’s done,’ Ed said and soon the boys were walking a short way back along the beach with their newfound friends. The men stopped at a spot that they seemed to recognise and began to gather driftwood to light a fire at their chosen spot. They laid down their coats for the boys to sit on next to the fire and then started to prepare their gear, finally separating to fish their own areas thereby ensuring they didn’t get tangled up with each other.

The boys started to get sleepy now they had been fed and watered. The heat from the fire added to their doziness. About an hour passed before there was a shout from Ed. The others immediately put down their rods and grabbed a net to help Ed land his catch. The boys could see a lot of splashing in the light reflected from the fire and soon the fishermen were walking back to the fire with a large pollack in their net.

It was still flapping away but that was soon stopped by Sam who gave it a crack over the head with a rock from the beach.

They left the fish for the boys to watch. 'Keep the rats away from the fish,' Sam said as they went back to their fishing. The boys looked at each other and huddled closer, throwing another piece of wood on the fire, worried they were going to be attacked by rats. Both had a stone in their hands ready to throw should a rat appear.

And so the night wore on. More fish were caught including an impressive flat fish called a plaice and a large cod.

By around 4am as the first slivers of light started to appear in the East, the fishermen decided to call it a day and came back to the fire. More sandwiches appeared as if by magic and the whiskey was passed around, apart from the boys, to warm the cockles of their hearts, as Ed explained.

The men then started to talk and the boys listened in fascination. All had been in the armed services in some shape or form. Ed had been in the navy and had spent most of the war escorting convoys across the Atlantic, He lived in Portland and many of his trips had started right here, next to where he lived. Sam had been a desert rat and had fought in Africa and then Sicily and Italy until the end of the war. Ray had been in the parachute regiment and had fought his way through Europe after landing in France on D-Day in June 1944.

The stories they shared of heroic deeds and friends they had lost amazed and saddened the boys in equal measure.

As they spoke, the sun broke the horizon and the fire gradually died out, the faint morning breeze scattering the ashes amongst the pebbles.

'Right, time to go home,' Sam finally announced, and the men got up and started to stow their kit and divide up the catch. Each had a stout sack and their portion of the catch was stowed in the sacks and shouldered by the fishermen.

'What are you doing today?' Sam asked the boys.

'Guess we'll need to head towards Weymouth,' PC suggested.

'You can come back to mine for some breakfast if you like,' Sam offered

'That would be lovely,' PC replied enthusiastically.

'And we'll put some iodine and a proper dressing on that wound.'

PC pulled a face at that, remembering having cuts and grazes dressed using iodine before.

Sam laughed and turned to walk along the beach towards Portland and his home, accompanied by his two friends with the boys following along.

'Our stuff!' Harry suddenly yelled out and ran up the beach as they passed the fishermen's huts where their night had started.

He came back down with their two bags and the much-travelled football. The friends smiled at each other and chased after the three fishermen.

Chapter Ten

It was three more days before Christine could organise another search. In the meantime, she had posted a report in a couple of the south coast papers about the missing boys to see if that elicited a response.

When they had searched around Chard they managed to track down the farm where the boys had stayed. Both Bill and Jean were pleased to hear that the boys seemed to be making their way safely and asked to be kept informed if they were found.

Now Sister Christine was leading them towards Charmouth to see if the boys had gone in that direction and to see if they were still there or if they had moved on.

The two jeeps pulled up in the car park down by the beach and the four of them got out and looked around.

'Where do we start?' Catherine asked.

'What are all those people doing?' Derek asked absentmindedly as he looked across at the people wandering around the beach.

'They're fossil hunting.' Christine stated. 'Why don't you go over and ask them if they have seen the boys?' Christine suggested to Karl and Derek. 'We'll head back into town and ask around.'

With that they split up, Karl and Derek heading off to the beach while the girls walked up the main street. There were a few fossil shops and coffee shops and they began asking after Harry and PC to see if anyone had seen them. In one shop the owner remembered the two boys and mentioned they had come in with a lady called Rita. He pointed back toward the beach and suggested they look for her there.

‘Look out for the tramp lady,’ the shopkeeper shouted to them as they left the shop.

Christine and Catherine looked at each other puzzled but headed back down to the beach to help the two GI’s with the search. They could see Karl and Derek talking to people as they combed the beach. One older lady stood out, she was a bit further along the beach and was bent over almost double as she turned stones, searching for the elusive fossils. The girls headed over to her, as they approached, she didn’t look up.

‘What do you want?’

‘Sorry to disturb you,’ Christine replied politely. ‘We are looking for two young boys and a man in one of the fossil shops says he saw you with two young lads a few days ago?’

‘He should mind his own business!’ Rita replied gruffly. ‘What do you want with them lads?’

‘We’re worried about them; they were in our care at the hospital where we work when they ran away, and we want to make sure they are OK.’

‘You should have looked after them better then.’ Rita muttered without looking up.

Catherine looked cross but Christine persisted. ‘Were they alright when you saw them?’

Rita finally stood up and looked at the girls.

‘They were fine lass, two really grand lads.’ Rita smiled. ‘My names Rita by the way and who might you be?’

‘My name is Sister Christine, and this is my colleague, Nurse Catherine.’

‘Well girls, I suggest you pop up to the George Inn and ask for Edith. She took to them right proper she did, even put them up for a night in her hotel. She can tell you all about them.’

‘Thank you so much,’ Christine said with a smile. ‘We’ll let you know how they are when we find them.’

‘Thank you for that, I hope you find them safe and sound, they are good boys, I just hope they remember me.’

‘I am sure they will,’ Christine replied. ‘Good luck with your fossil hunt.’

With that they waved to Karl and Derek to come over and together they walked back into town and up to the George Inn. Once they found the hotel, Christine suggested the boys go back and get the jeeps while they spoke to the Edith. Christine knocked on the door. Edith answered the door and immediately invited them in. She took them through to the small lounge and offered them a cup of tea.

‘A coffee would be nice,’ Catherine replied.

‘Sorry, I don’t have any I’m afraid, rationing and all that. Tea then?’

‘That would be lovely.’ Christine replied, knowing how important the tea ritual was to the British.

The girls sat in silence, apart from the ticking of a grandfather clock, while Edith brewed up the tea, taking in the pretty room and the myriad ornaments and such like that surrounded them.

Eventually Edith returned with a teapot on a tray. The teapot was covered in a woollen tea cosy and was accompanied by three china cups, which didn’t match. She had also found a few biscuits to offer the girls and they politely took their cups and a biscuit each.

‘Are you trying to find Harry and Peter,’ Edith offered with a little smile.

Christine almost choked on her tea. ‘That’s very perceptive or is it that obvious?’

‘Well nothing much happens around here and when two things happen in a couple of days, it’s pretty likely that the two are related.’

Edith smiled and sipped her tea.

Christine put her cup down and her half-eaten biscuit.

‘The boys broke out of the hospital while we were caring for them. We are worried that they weren’t ready to leave and just want to know if they are OK. We also want to make sure they get home safely.’

Edith sipped her tea again,

‘You shouldn’t have decided to split them up,’ Edith suggested. ‘You know they are devoted to each other and you were going to break that bond.’

‘Hindsight is a wonderful thing I guess, but you are right. We should have spotted that and kept them together then none of this would have happened.’

Christine picked up her teacup and cradled it in her hands. Catherine put her hand on Christine’s shoulder as her friend started to cry.

‘I am just so worried about them.’ Christine said quietly.

Edith could see the care the girls felt for the boys and tried to reassure them.

‘They were fine and healthy when they left here. They had eaten well and even had money in their pockets from fossils they had found on the beach with Rita.’

‘Do you know where they were going?’ Catherine asked.

Edith thought for a moment.

‘They were going to aim for Abbotsbury and then head on to Weymouth. I told them to avoid the beach so they would have headed along the path on top of the cliffs.’

Christine thought for a moment. She turned to Catherine ‘Well we can’t take the jeeps over the fields, so we’ll have to find a way to Abbotsbury and see if anyone has seen them there. Thank you for all your help Edith, and for the tea. I’ll let you know when we find them, and we really appreciate you looking after them. They have been very lucky to have met so many nice people on their journey.’

Edith leaned over and squeezed Christine’s arm. ‘And thank you for caring so much about them dear.’

The girls quickly finished their tea and headed out to the jeeps. After a quick update for Karl and Derek they headed back up through the town and turned towards Abbotsbury.

When they pulled into the town they asked around. No-one seemed to have seen the boys, so they headed down to the swannery and were soon taking to Philip. He walked them up the farmhouse and soon the girls were talking to Leanne who explained that they had stayed with them and headed off along Chesil Beach two days ago.

Sister Christine took their details and promised to keep in touch and let them know if they found the boys. Time was getting on and for all they knew the boys could be back in the Channel Islands by now. They reluctantly decided to head back to Taunton and in convoy they drove out of Abbotsbury.

Christine knew they were close but just not close enough.

When they got back to Taunton a note was waiting for Sister Christine. It was from a lady in Portland. The boys were with her.

Sister Christine burst into tears with relief. Catherine rushed in to find out what was wrong.

'They're safe,' Christine explained through her tears. Catherine put her arm around her friend's shoulders and she too shed a tear. They stayed like that for a minute before Christine recovered her composure.

'Come on Catherine, I need your help. We have some planning to do,' Christine smiled, wiping the tears from her eyes.

Chapter Eleven

It wasn't long before they were walking off the beach and heading into what the boys later learned was the lovely named little town of Fortuneswell.

The men split up and went their separate ways and the boys walked with Sam up the High Street until they arrived at his little end of terrace cottage. The front door was unlocked and opened straight into a small front room with a staircase in the corner and a door through to the kitchen.

'Is that you love,' a voice called out from the kitchen.

A small woman leaned back from the sink to see who had just come in. She had long brown hair tied back with a scarf. She had a beautiful smile, dimpled rosy cheeks and very red hands. She wore a light blue pinafore which was wet in patches as she had been washing a few clothes. She smiled at Sam and looked quizzically at the two young boys he had brought home with him.

'Look what I caught on the beach Ruth,' Sam said smiling.

'Not your usual catch love,' Ruth replied drying her hands on the cloth hanging from the waist of her pinny.

'Wipe your feet you three and then you two boys sit down. I bet you could do with some breakfast,' she said walking up to Sam and giving him a kiss on the cheek. She then sniffed his bag and wrinkled her nose. 'And you can put those fish out the back and get yourself cleaned up.'

The boys gave the doormat a vigorous brushing with their shoes then put their bags down in a corner of the room behind the front door. They then took a seat at a small table which took up the opposite corner of the lounge next to the door to the kitchen.

Sam followed Ruth through to the kitchen and whispered something in her ear and then went out into the backyard. He was soon back in the kitchen and took over washing the clothes while Ruth opened a cupboard and brought a neat little box into the front room.

'Sam tells me you caught your leg on a fish hook my dear, can I have a look?'

PC looked a little nervous but held out his leg so she could have a look at the small wound.

She knelt in front of him, placing his foot in her lap. She gently took off the temporary bandage Sam had tied around his leg and then ran her hand around his calf, checking for any swelling. 'Sam did a good job,' she said more to herself than to PC.

'The best thing I can do for this Peter is to give it a dab of iodine and a fresh bandage, are you OK with that?'

PC nodded, wondering how she knew his name.

She opened the small tin and got out a small vial of iodine and a piece of clean cloth. She poured a small amount on the cloth and then dabbed it on the two small puncture wounds. PC winced a little but in truth it hardly hurt at all. She then got a small roll of bandage and wound it around his calf, making sure it was tight enough not to fall down then she cut the bandage, before splitting the bandage from the cut end enough to enable her to tie the ends around his leg, securing the bandage firmly in place.

She leaned back to admire her handiwork. 'That should keep the wound clean until it is properly healed up, just leave it on for the next couple of days and you'll be fine.'

As she looked at his leg, she noticed some fresh scars on his other leg but didn't say anything.

PC thanked her for the treatment and Ruth went back into the kitchen and started to make breakfast for them all.

PC leaned over to Harry who seemed fascinated to see Sam doing the washing. 'How did she know my name?'

'Sam must have told her,' Harry replied without looking away from the kitchen door.

'But we didn't tell him my proper name, all he ever knew was that you called me PC?'

Harry turned to PC and cocked his head for a second, deep in thought. 'You're right, maybe it was a guess?'

'Good guess,' PC replied quietly.

They sat for a while watching the action in the kitchen and before long the delicious smell of bacon and eggs was followed by two plates of food for the boys who devoured their breakfasts greedily. Hot cups of tea followed and soon the boys were full and happy. They were also quite sleepy after a busy night on the beach, so Ruth suggested they snuggle down on the small settee suite and have a nap.

She cleared the dishes away and went into the kitchen, closing the door quietly not to disturb the boys.

She joined Sam in the back yard where he was hanging out the washing.

'It's definitely them,' she said to Sam.

'Yep,' what do you think we should do?

'Well the newspaper said we should let the hospital know if we see them so I guess we should do that.'

‘I’m not so sure,’ Sam said quietly. ’I think they are just trying to get home and they have got this far and seem pretty fit and well. I respect that!’

He thought for a moment. ‘I need some sleep too so let’s wait until we can have a proper chat with them and see what they say. Are you happy with that?’

Ruth looked back at the house and pictured the two friends sound asleep, safe and sound.

‘OK, let’s wait until this afternoon. You get some sleep; I need to go to work. I promise I won’t say anything.’

With that she went back into the house and changed into her nurses uniform, she then went into the back yard, pulled her bike out of the shed, pushed it through the back gate and rode off towards the Portland Naval Hospital, where she worked.

Sam tiptoed back through the front room, locked the front door and then went up the stairs to get some sleep. The boys were sound asleep, and he would soon follow. The Western Morning News carrying the article about the missing boys lay on a small table next to Sam’s armchair.

*****

It was around noon when Harry woke up. A noise in the road outside the cottage had disturbed his sleep and he walked across to look outside, gently pulling aside the net curtains to see more clearly. A small bread van was making its way down the road, stopping at the occasional cottage to deliver bread. He looked back at PC who was still sound asleep. Apart from the ticking of the clock on the mantelpiece and the dripping of the tap in the kitchen the house was in silence.

Rather than disturb PC he sat in the armchair by the fireplace and took stock of his surroundings. It was a neat room with a couple of lovely photos of Ruth and Sam above the fireplace.

One was of Sam in his uniform and Ruth in civilian clothes at their wedding. Another was of the two of them on the beach in bathers, both smiling and happy. He noted there were no photos of children anywhere, but he guessed they may not have been married long so maybe they would have children one day. He decided he needed the toilet so popped into the back yard and found the loo then, after he was finished, he washed his hands under an outside tap he found above a drain.

He walked back into the cottage, taking stock of the small kitchen this time. He took a cup off the draining board and filled it at the tap and took a long drink of water. He filled it again and took it with him back into the front room. He again sat in the armchair and went to put the cup down on the small table, moving the paper so as to not get it wet. His eyes went over the paper as he lifted it up and there on the front page was a small article about two missing boys. Peter Cochrane and Harry Carre. 'That's how she knew PC's name,' he thought to himself.

He read the rest of the article including the request for anyone seeing the boys to contact Musgrove Park Hospital in Taunton. Harry thought for a while and then got up and gently shook PC by the shoulder until he woke up. As his friend woke up, he put his fingers to his lips to tell him to keep quite and then handed him the paper to read.

PC straightened up and read the article before giving the paper back to Harry.

'What shall we do?'

'I don't know,' Harry replied quietly, 'maybe we should get away before they call the hospital and they come to get us.'

'Maybe you're right,'

They went over to pick up their bags and the football and went to the front door. Harry turned the handle as quietly as he could and tried to open the door, but it was firmly locked.
He gave it another rattle, but it wouldn't budge.

'There's a back gate,' Harry suggested.

The two boys turned back towards the kitchen, but Sam was standing half way down the stairs looking at them.

'Leaving without saying goodbye boys?' Sam said smiling. 'Now that's not very polite.'

'Sorry,' PC offered.

'We need to get home Sam,' Harry said urgently. 'Our families will be wondering where we are.'

'Now that's a bit of a lie now isn't it? Sam said more seriously. 'So, before we go making any rash decisions why don't we have a cup of tea and wait until Ruth gets back home and then we can all talk about what we should do next.'

'OK,' Harry said quietly, and the boys put their bags and the football back in the corner and sat back on the sofa while Sam put the kettle on and brewed tea for them all.

The silence was a little awkward to say the least so Sam suggested he show the boys how to gut and prepare fish. This seemed to break the ice and once the tea was drunk, they trooped out to the shed in the back yard and Sam got out his fish knife and the catch from the night before. The pollack he caught first was laid out on the slab and he gently showed the boys where to cut. He lifted the fin on the side of the body just behind its head and placed the knife there and then cut down, severing the head from the body. He then put the knife into the belly of the fish and cut back towards the tail. The stomach and innards were then scrapped out and put to one side. He took the gutted body of the fish across to the drain and rinsed out any leftover blood under the tap and then came back to create the fillets.

He gently found the backbone with his knife and slid it along the backbone towards the tail, creating a lovely clean plump fillet. He turned the fish over and repeated the process. The boys were fascinated.

Two other fish were given the same treatment and soon 6 lovely fillets were prepared.

'We'll have one each for tea,' he announced and getting a tea towel from the kitchen wrapped them all and placed them on the work top next to the sink.

'Are you wondering what we do with the heads and bits and pieces?' The thought hadn't crossed their mind, but PC nodded, and they all went back to the shed. Sam placed the heads, backbones and innards on an old newspaper and took them outside. He then threw them up on to the shed roof.

'Now watch this,' he said and pulled them back just inside the back door.

Within 30 seconds a seagull started circling above the cottage and next thing two more flew in across the rooftops and landed on the shed roof. Soon there were over half a dozen of the big birds fighting for the fish pieces and within two minutes the roof was clear.

The boys were amazed.

'Fancy peeling a few potatoes boys?' Sam suggested, breaking the spell the boys were under after the spectacle.

Soon the kitchen was a hive of activity with vegetables boiling away and fish frying in a pan on top of the aga.

Ruth came home just before 6 and tea was ready and waiting for her.

Sam pulled the table out from the corner and soon they were all sitting around enjoying their tea. Ruth talked about her day and how busy she was at the hospital. There were still several servicemen in the hospital recovering from injuries sustained during the war and in accidents that had happened since.

As the meal came to an end Sam explained to Ruth that the boys knew that they had read about them in the newspaper. He then gave them the chance to tell their story.

PC looked at Harry who indicated that he was happy for PC to do the talking.

PC then took them through the whole story. He explained how they had hurt each other playing football and had missed the organised trip back to the Channel Islands. Then he explained how they had made their escape as soon as they felt fit enough to do so and how they had found their way to Chesil Beach via Chard, Axminster and Charmouth.

The couple listened to the story in silence but when PC stopped, Ruth asked what they planned to do next.

Harry stepped in at this point.

'We were hoping to get across to Weymouth and get on one of the ferries back to the Islands,' he looked at PC, 'and we nearly made it.'

The boys looked down at their empty plates and a single tear ran down PC's face.

'We just want to go home,' he said, his voice trembling.

Ruth reached across and held PC's hand. She looked at Sam and he nodded.

'We won't give you up boys,' she said quietly. 'Stay with us for a couple of days and when this is old news, we'll get you to Weymouth. Once you are on the boat, I'll let the Hospital know you are safe and on your way home. Is that OK?'

The boys couldn't believe their luck. 'Thank you so much,' they said in unison. 'That's really OK,' PC added with a big smile.

'Right, now you need to earn your keep. Give me a hand with the dishes and then maybe you can go with Sam tonight and see if you can catch us some tea for tomorrow. I need to get some sleep.'

The boys laughed and headed into the kitchen.

'Thanks Ruth,' Sam said leaning over and giving her a kiss. 'They're lovely boys and are in safe hands here.'

'I know, just don't go getting them caught on any fishhooks tonight or we'll both be in trouble, but there is something I think we should do. I'll explain later.'

Soon it was all hands to the pumps and the dishes were cleared away while Sam went out into the shed to get two more fishing rods ready for the boys to use that night. Ruth popped out to help him and told him her plan. He agreed with her idea and gave her a big hug.

By 9.30pm they were all packed up and ready to go. Some bits of last night's catch that hadn't been given to the seagulls were prepared as bait, sandwiches were wrapped up, flasks of tea were filled up and lamps were lit. The three of them loaded up with rods, nets, bags and lights, then after hugs from Ruth and a kiss for Sam they were off down the road towards Chesil beach.

Ruth waved them off until they had disappeared from sight and then headed off to bed. She noticed the football in the corner and out of curiosity picked it up and gave it a closer look. She noted it was looking a bit battered and patchy, which she imagined must be salt from a soaking in the sea. She could also see that some of the panels had signatures on them and realised that other people had met the boys at some point in the past and had signed the ball. She looked around and found a fountain pen and carefully signed her name on an empty panel.

She placed it back down where she had found it and with a smile, climbed up the stairs to bed.

Sam and the boys took the same route down to the beach as they had when they came off the beach the night before. Soon they were crunching along the pebbles as the sun slowly set in the West. Sam kept looking across to the cliffs and at a particular mark, where he had no doubt fished before, he announced that this was the spot.

Harry and PC took a few steps up the beach to make a camp with all their gear while Sam readied the first of the rods so as not to waste any fishing time. Soon the first bait was cast out into the sea and the rod was fixed on a stand and a small bell was placed next to the tip to signal if any fish were showing an interest in the bait. Sam then helped the boys get their rigs sorted out, showing them how to tie the hooks on to the line, how to shape the rig so that the weight was last on the line so that the bait could float free further up the line. Sam called it a three-way rig.

He showed the boys how to tie the line to the hook using a knot he called a clinch knot. He told them he would always spit on the knot to make it slide tight against the hook and for luck. The boys had fun practising their knots before Sam was sure they were making knots that would hold if they caught a decent sized fish.

Then it was casting practice. This was a bit more complicated. PC seemed to take to it much quicker than Harry but soon it turned into a competition as to who could cast the line the furthest.

Sam sat back and smiled as he watched them play together. He was silently hoping he would have his own boys one day to pass his knowledge too, the same way his Dad had taught him.

Once he was happy the rods and reels were being used properly, the lines were baited up and with Harry standing to his left and PC to his right they cast their rods, stood them on their stands and once their bells were attached, came back and sat with Sam to see if the fish would bite.

The three were well wrapped up against the chill of the night and huddled together they didn't notice the temperature dropping.

'What was it like in Africa?' Harry asked Sam.

'Hot as hell,' Sam replied with a smile. 'Left a lot of good mates out there thanks to Rommel.'

'Where abouts were you?' PC asked.

'All over,' Sam replied almost reluctantly. 'Sidi Barrani, El Alamein, Tobruk, I saw them all. Managed to get through it all with just a few scratches. I was very lucky,' he added wistfully as if the memories were flooding back. 'I don't like to talk about it.' Sam added emphatically.

Suddenly and thankfully the ensuing silence was broken by Sam's rod bending over and the bell jingling like mad as a fish took his bait and headed out to sea.

'Quick, reel your lines in to make sure we don't get tangled up.'

The boys sprang into action and soon they were standing and watching Sam as he battled the fish.

'PC grab the net,' Sam shouted as he fought the fish. 'This is a biggun.'

The boys were amazed as Sam struggled with the fish and were shocked at the scream of the reel as the fish occasionally gained ground and took line out. After what seemed an age but was in effect around ten minutes, the fish broke surface with a loud splash and the boys knew the battle was nearly won. PC edged down into the water with the net and as Sam gave the fish a last tug it drifted over the net allowing PC to lift the net around the fish. Sam immediately dropped the rod and grabbed the net, heaving the fish out of the water and carrying it a few steps up the beach. In the light of one of the lamps, a beautiful bass of around 20lb in weight lay looking up at them. Sam took a rock from the bank of pebbles and cracked it over the head, killing it outright.

'Wow, what a great fish,' Sam said, still breathing heavily from the fight. 'I've never caught one as big as that, you must be lucky charms.'

The boys smiled up at Sam, but a bit of PC regretted that the fish had to die. It looked so beautiful in the light, but he felt sad as its eyes gradually glazed over and the life drained out of the creature. Eventually Sam lifted it up and took it further up the beach to drop it into his sack ready to take home. PC's mind drifted to those far off battle fields and imagined the men who had also lost their lives and how they too must have felt as their time had come, as their eyes glazed over and their lives drifted away. A tear escaped his eyes and ran down his cheek and he quickly wiped it away before anyone noticed.

His reverie was broken as Harry started to get his fishing gear together and cast out his line to try and emulate Sam's success. 'Come on PC, let's see if we can catch one,' he shouted up the beach.

Almost reluctantly PC got up from where he was sitting and before long, he too had cast out his line as Sam busied himself resetting his bait to try and add to his catch for the night.

It would be another hour before they had any more luck and this time it was Harry's rod that bent over, the bell ringing furiously. He fought to bring his fish home but was unlucky when the line snapped, and the fish broke free before it could be landed. Harry was amazed at the feeling that he got through the rod. He could feel the fish struggling on the line and was literally hooked on fishing from that moment on. He tried to describe it to PC, but words couldn't explain how catching a fish felt.

Harry trudged up the beach to tie a new hook and weight to his line and while he was away Sam's rod received a bite and this time the fish didn't seem to put up as much of a fight. Sam offered to hand PC the rod so he could feel the fish on the line, but PC declined. He was secretly hoping he didn't catch anything that night and had quietly reeled his bait in to nearer the shore in the hope the fish wouldn't come that close.

This time Sam brought ashore a nice pollack which was dispatched in the same way as the bass, then it too ended up in Sam's fish sack.

At about 2 in the morning Sam noticed PC yawning away and as they had two nice fish, he decided to call it a night and head home. Soon they were making their way across the pebbles heading back to Sam's cottage in Fortuneswell.

The boys were soon asleep, and it seemed no time at all before they were woken by the smell of bacon and eggs wafting through the cottage. It turns out it was Ruth's day off and she was cooking a late breakfast for 'her boys' as she called them, as a treat.

All four tucked into the meal and while they did, they made some plans for the day.

It was agreed that the four of them would take a walk down to Portland Lighthouse. Harry asked if they could take the fishing rods, but Ruth was firmly of the mind that this would not involve any fishing. However, she had prepared the pollack and fried fish sandwiches would form part of a picnic they would take with them. The weather looked set fair for the day so light clothes were in order. Ruth managed to rustle up a few bits and pieces so the boys could wear something different to the clothes they had been wearing since they left the hospital. She put those to soak while they were out so she could wash them properly when they got back.

Soon they were off on their way south towards the lighthouse, Sam carrying a basket full of food and lemonade in one hand and holding Ruth's hand with the other and the two boys kicking PC's football backwards and forwards as they made their way along the quiet roads. Occasionally Sam would have a kick and even Ruth managed a not too bad effort when the ball rolled her way. Smiles were the order of the day as the four made their way along Wide Street and then Weston Road. From time to time the couple would see someone they knew and would exchange hellos and on one occasion they stopped for a brief chat.

Soon they were through Weston and Southwell and on the last stretch down Portland Bill Road. They could see the lighthouse ahead and were soon walking past the Coastguard cottages and the huts which people used as summer holiday accommodation, a few had bathers and towels hanging outside them to show they were in use.

Then they were walking around the lighthouse and gazing in awe at the size of the building. They walked past it right to the seas edge and a small area where they could look out across the English Channel towards France and of course the Channel Islands.

‘This is the closest you can get to home boys without getting on a boat. Can you smell home?’ Sam asked, smiling.

The boys both took a deep breath and turned to the couple. ‘Oh yes,’ they said in unison. ‘It smells of the sea,’ PC added.

They all laughed, and another kick around started as Ruth sat on a rock and nursed the picnic basket.

Sam was in goal and the boys did their best to kick the ball past him. Eventually it all got a bit too enthusiastic and a shot by Harry flew over Sam’s head and over the cliff edge.

They all ran over and watched as PC’s precious football tumbled down across the rocks and settled in a rockpool.

They looked around to try and find a way down and after a while found a place where Sam could lower one of the boys down to the beach level. Despite Ruth’s protestations PC was lowered over the edge of the rocks and dropped a few feet down to the lower level so he could carefully head over to where the ball was floating. He felt a bit of a twinge as he landed but tested his leg and it seemed alright. *Must be healing well*, he thought to himself.

He managed to gather the ball without falling in and deftly kicked it back up to the top of the cliff where Harry caught it. He gave it to Ruth to look after as they debated how to get PC back up the cliff.

Harry and Sam split up and followed the cliff edge around until Harry found a rough path and directed PC around to it so he could make his way up. Sam came across and between the two of them they pulled PC up the last few feet to the top of the cliff.

‘Phew, that was close,’ PC panted. ‘Nearly lost the ball.’

'Nearly lost you, silly boys.' Ruth commented with a stern look. She had noticed PC was limping a bit. 'How's your leg?'

'Feels OK,' PC replied. 'Just gave it a bit of a jolt when I landed.'

'Well that was a stupid thing to do boys,' she said, addressing all of them. 'Let's go and have this picnic while there are still four of us to eat it. And no more football, Peter needs to rest,' she added.

The boys looked sheepishly at each other and Sam hurried to pick up the picnic basket as they headed off to find a nice sunny spot to enjoy their lunch. They followed the coastal path along towards the huts and eventually settled on a flat piece of grass where they could rest their backs against a rocky outcrop and enjoy the sun. Soon the picnic blanket was laid out and all were tucking into their fried fish sandwiches, apples and homemade lemonade, a real treat so soon after the war.

After lunch they sat and talked for a while, the boys sharing stories of their respective home Islands and from time to time Sam and Ruth would find them gazing quietly towards the horizon no doubt thinking of what lay in wait for them under those distant clouds.

Sam fell asleep for a while with Ruth resting on his shoulder. All was well with their world.

After about an hour Ruth announced that they should be heading home and suggested they follow the coast around the eastern edge of Portland so the boys could see all the defences that had been built to fend off the anticipated German attacks. The boys were keen on the idea and soon everything was packed away. Sam picked up the much lighter basket for the journey home, pulling Ruth to her feet with his free hand. They headed off past the huts, retracing their outward journey until they turned off onto the Southwell Road and headed towards Rufus Castle, or the Bow and Arrow Castle as Ruth called it.

They then walked past the imposing Borstal, where Sam insisted they would end up if they misbehaved. Ruth mentioned that it had been bombed during the war and some of the boys had been killed which quietened the boys much more than the threats of incarceration from Sam

They turned off the road and took a path that was closer to the sea. They spotted several sand lizards scampering away from them and the boys started a competition to see who could see the most. As they rounded a bend in the path the impressive expanse of Portland harbour opened up in front of them.

When they reached the historic batteries at East Weare they could see across Portland harbour to Weymouth, the boy's final destination in England on their journey home. As if on cue, a passenger ship headed out of the harbour and headed south towards the islands. Ruth took a boy under each arm.

'Soon boys, that will be you,' a single tear running down her face.

Sam put his arm around her shoulder knowing what she was thinking. The boys remained quiet, each thinking of their journey and the amazing people they had met and of course, what waited for them at home.

After the ship had sailed into the distance, they turned towards the Verne Citadel, another historic defence on Portland. They headed across some fields and open land with Ruth leading the way and were soon back on the road and heading down into Fortuneswell and home.

The boys had thoroughly enjoyed their day and it was decided there would be no fishing that night as they were well stocked and everyone needed a good night's sleep as Ruth was back to work tomorrow. She was soon busy washing their clothes and getting them ready so they could wear them the next day and over a light tea it was agreed Sam would do some research the next day to find out the ferry times and check how they could get home.

Both boys didn't sleep well that night as they pondered leaving England and how lovely it was here with Ruth and Sam. While they tossed and turned Ruth showed Sam the football and got him to sign a panel.

'I wish they were our boys,' she confessed to Sam.

'I know, I feel the same, they would make any parent proud.'

'Do you think we will see them again?' Ruth asked quietly.

'We'll make sure we do. I've always fancied a trip to the Channel Islands and let's face it they are only just out of sight.'

Ruth smiled and snuggled into Sam, dreaming of the day they had their own children and of boat trips to the islands to see the boys.

She was almost asleep when Sam shook her gently. 'Come on, let's go to bed.'

He stood up and pulled Ruth to her feet, kissing her tenderly as she reached her full height. Soon they were in bed and unlike the boys they were asleep as soon as their heads hit the pillow.

*****

The next day the boys woke up late. There was no bacon and eggs smell to make their mouths water today but when they got to the breakfast table some bread and jam was waiting for them with lots of real butter. Sam was waiting for them and had the kettle boiling so he could make them some tea. Ruth had already left for work.

'Good morning sleepy heads.' Sam smiled as he poured the tea and got the boys settled around the table.

Soon they were tucking into strawberry jam sandwiches and slurping piping hot tea.

'What do you fancy doing today?' Sam asked as they enjoyed their breakfast.

The boys both shrugged their shoulders as they munched away at their second sandwich. PC gulped down his mouthful and asked what there was to do.

'Well, we could go fishing,' Sam suggested. Harry seemed keen but PC didn't look to enthusiastic.

Seeing PC's face, he paused for a second to have a think. 'Or how about a run out in a boat?'

The boys looked at each other and nodded enthusiastically.

'Right then,' Sam announced loudly slapping his knees and getting up from the table. 'Let's see if we can hitch a ride with one of my friends.'

The boys rushed off to clean their teeth and go to the loo before they set off on their next adventure.

Soon they were heading off across Portland towards the Weymouth side and down to a small cove just below Portland Castle where several small boats were moored. Sam called out to a fisherman who was mending nets down on the jetty as they started walking down the steps. 'Heh Mick, how is life treating you?' Sam smiled as he continued down the steps to the jetty followed by the boys.

'I'm alright,' Mick replied remaining focused on his nets. 'What brings you here?'

'I've got some friends with me and they'd like a trip out in a boat. Are you going out later to do some fishing?'

‘Aye, that I am. When I’ve finished repairing this net. I caught a giant shark in it recently and it ripped a big hole in the net while t was trying to get free.’

‘Shark,’ PC blurted out. ‘How big was it?’

Mick looked up for the first time.

‘Hello lad,’ he looked PC and Harry up and down. ‘I reckon it was twice the size of you. It could have eaten you in just a few bites.’

He went back to his nets as Sam burst out laughing. The boys were in a state of shock and turned to look at Sam. ‘He’s just messing with you.’ Sam said laughing.

Mick spoke while weaving his thread through the net. ‘Believe what you like boys but it is always good to have a healthy respect for the sea because you never know what might be under the water.’

He worked on for a few moments. ‘Do you still want to come out in my boat?’

The boys both nodded. ‘Speak up boys, I need to know you will always be ready to talk if you get into trouble. I also need you to know that I am Captain of my boat so if you come with me you must always do as I say. Fishing boats are dangerous vessels, full of sharp and dangerous things. Men who have sailed the seas all their lives have been killed for one lapse in concentration. Are you still happy to come with me?’

‘Yes Captain,’ the boys replied.

‘Good,’ Captain Mick responded getting up from the crab pot he was sitting on and using a large knife he cut the line he was using to mend the net and tied it off. ‘Then let’s get going.’

‘Sam, you and the boys get the dinghy ready. Chop, chop,’ he added, waving his knife in the direction of the small boat tied to the jetty.

Sam ushered the boys down some weed covered steps.

‘Be careful,’ Mick shouted, just as Harry slipped.

Thankfully Sam grabbed him by the shoulder before he could fall. Harry reached out and caught hold of the rusty railing which was attached to the jetty wall to steady himself. PC hurriedly followed suit and gingerly they made their way down to the waiting dinghy. Sam climbed in first and then held out a hand for the boys to help them on board.

Mick appeared above them and began passing down the net. The boys sat still in the back of the dinghy while Sam caught hold of the net and stowed it in the bow of the boat. Once he had it all carefully packed away, he sat on it and loosened the bow rope where it was tied to the steps ready for departure. Mick then made his way down and climbed on to the centre seat looking straight at the boys with his back to Sam. The sea in the cove was flat calm and looked beautiful as the sun beat down warming their skin and bringing a smile to their faces.

Mick scowled at them. Harry was closest to the wall so Mick pointed to him, ‘You, undo that knot holding the stern to the wall. And don’t fall into the water?’

‘My names Harry, Captain,’ Harry replied bravely. He leaned over the back of the boat, PC held the back of his shirt as he did, and after a bit of a struggle he managed to loosen the rope and bring it on board.

Mick grunted and with one oar pushed them away from the steps and then began rowing them out to sea.

PC looked a bit puzzled and eventually asked a question.

‘I thought the boat would be bigger than this?’

Captain Mick and Sam both roared with laughter.

‘This is a dinghy boy, my boat is out there,’ he explained pointing behind him with a nod of his head.

The boys tried to look past Captain Mick and Sam, but they couldn’t really see where they were heading but Mick seemed to know the way even though he wasn’t looking where he was going.

After about ten minutes a large fishing boat with a red hull appeared in front of the dinghy and before long they were tying up alongside. PC noted the scratches and rust streaks down the side. Across the top of the wheelhouse was the name Silver Fox. Mick took the bow rope from Sam and stood up grabbing the handrail of the boat as he did. Sam stood up too grabbing the side of the boat and moved back from the bow to hold the dinghy tight to the boat as Mick climbed aboard. He then lent over and offered the boys a hand. First PC and then Harry were helped over the side on to the deck of the fishing boat. Both stayed where they were too terrified to move in case they got in the way.

Sam then passed the net to Mick and he hauled it on board before Sam deftly pulled himself on to the Silver Fox to complete their crew for the day.

The fishing boat was just over 24 feet long with a small stern cabin, a mast at the front of the boat and a smaller one behind the cabin. Mick walked to the front of the boat and tied the dinghy to the same large buoy the Silver Fox was tied to. He then lifted a panel on the floor to reveal an old diesel engine. He leaned into the engine compartment and primed the engine before pulling a rope to start it. After a few pulls the well-oiled old diesel kicked into life and with a low chugging noise turned over steadily. Mick replaced the panel and asked Sam to cast off from the buoy.

Once Sam had freed the boat from the buoy, Mick reversed the boat away from the buoy before heading off out to sea leaving their dinghy bobbing away in the gentle swell, slowly disappearing into the distance.

While Sam chatted with Mick in the small wheelhouse of the Silver Fox, the boys sat in the sun in front of the wheelhouse, enjoying the warmth on their faces as they chugged out to sea.

'Just think, next time we are on a boat, we will be on our way home,' PC commented, staring up a circling seagull.

Harry just nodded, staring wistfully into the distance.

PC thought he noticed tears in Harry's eyes and put his hand on his friend's knee. 'Are you OK?'

Harry nodded, looking at his friend.

'Just not sure I want to go home,' he said sadly.

PC thought for a moment.

'Don't you want to see Jersey again and see your family?' PC asked.

'Of course, I do,' Harry replied. 'But the people here have been so friendly and helpful, I will miss them so much.'

'I know,' PC replied thinking carefully.

'You know you will be able to visit again, and if you don't like it back in Jersey, I am sure someone here will take you in and look after you.' He paused for a moment to let Harry think about his words. 'Think of Sam and Ruth, Bill and Jean, Edith, John and of course Norma,' he said with a wink and a smile. 'Even Sister Christine and Nurse Catherine would help you find a home, maybe in America - you could become a cowboy,' he added with a laugh.

That got Harry laughing. They laughed so much Sam popped out to see if they were OK.

After about an hour's chugging the boys heard the engine note change as Mick slowed the boat and prepared to check his pots. Soon the boat came to a dead stop in the shadow of some cliffs and Sam grabbed a boat hook and soon was fishing the first pot out of the water. He shouted to the boys to help and soon they were all hauling on the line as the first of a string of crab pots bashed against the side of the boat. Sam leaned over and hauled the pot on board and Mick came forward with a large slatted wooden box. He reached into the crab pot and pulled out a large chancre crab. Two more smaller chancre crabs came out of the pot and were dropped into the box.

Five more pots made the journey on to the boat and another dozen crabs found their way into the pot. As a bonus the last crab pot contained a creature neither of the boys had seen before. It was a large lobster and Mick was overjoyed to see it and reckoned it would pay for his fuel for a week. He skillfully tied the large claws shut so it didn't damage the smaller crabs in the box and soon it too disappeared into the storage box.

Next, he and Sam, with the help of the boys started to pay out the fishing net they had brought with them. As soon as it was part way overboard, he headed back to the wheelhouse and gently eased the boat back to help pay the net out. Weights on one side and the glass buoys on the other separated the net out like a curtain. Soon it was all in the water and carefully Mick eased the boat around to create a circle with the net. Under the water the movement of the boat sent shoals of small fish towards the net and soon many were stuck halfway through the mesh, pinned by their gills.

When he was sure the net was ready, Mick shouted the order to pull and the four of them pulled the lines holding the ends of the net. The two boys were on one end and Sam and Mick on the other. Soon the net was near the side of the boat and the net was being pulled over the side. Loads of small fish were flapping in the net and on the deck. Seagulls started to circle overhead in ever increasing numbers as they sensed the chance of an easy meal.

Once the net was back on board, Mick started to gather the fish in a bucket, throwing some of them back overboard before they perished in the sun. Some of these were stunned and the hungry gulls dived down and picked the unlucky ones off the surface of the sea. The boys were shattered with the effort of the work and their hands were red from pulling the rope but they both smiled at their success and the fact they had kept up with the two men. Mick now had two buckets of fish. The boys were asked to spend time cleaning the net, pulling out any seaweed that was still caught up in the mesh. While they were doing that Mick started to gut the smaller fish and threaded them on to the wires in the crab pots. PC noticed and quickly turned away. He was growing to hate the killing of the fish, not that it made him feel sick, it was just the pain it inflicted on the fish.

Mick noticed PC was avoiding what he was doing and called him over.

‘A bit squeamish lad?’ Mick asked.

‘No Captain,’ PC replied keeping his eyes off the gutted fish in Mick’s bucket.

‘Then do you fancy helping me gut a few fish son?’

‘I’d rather not,’ PC replied. ‘It looks cruel to the fish.’

‘They don’t feel anything son,’ Mick assured him. ‘They’re cold blooded creatures and don’t feel things like we do.’

‘How do you know that Captain? PC replied. ‘Can you be sure?’

‘Well.’ Mick paused for a second. ‘Let’s put it this way, if it was OK for Jesus in the bible to feed the five thousand with bread and fish, then it must be OK.’

PC seemed unconvinced.

‘Let me show you the fascination of fish gutting,’ Mick offered. PC nodded cautiously as Mick picked a fish out of the bucket. By now they were all dead from being out of the water. ‘The reason I am doing this is that the crabs and lobsters like to eat fish, so the pots need to be baited with dead fish. The crabs and lobsters are attracted to the smell of the blood so by opening the fish up it helps speed up the process of attracting them to the pot.’

By now Harry had come over to listen and learn from the Captain.

Mick continued. ‘I’ll use my knife to cut the base of the fish here and slide it down towards the tail, that exposes the insides. If you ever go fishing it is always an idea to open any fish you catch to see what they are eating.’ He showed the boys how to open the stomach and see what the fish had to eat.

By this time PC had become fascinated, as was Harry and they took turns to cut open a fish and see what they could find inside.

As they were working Mick told them how he had caught a large shark once and when he opened it up, the sharks stomach contained a human hand. Both the boys were appalled. ‘Yuck!’ Harry yelled.

Behind them Sam was laughing like mad at their reaction. He had heard some of Mick’s tales before.

Before long all the crab pots were ready to go back in the water and Mick was soon back at the wheel piloting the boat back to his favourite mark. Sam and the boys launched them over the side of the boat as the line played out and once the final marker buoy was in the water Mick turned the boat and headed back to the small harbour and home.

This time the boys hung over the side of the boat, watching the water splash past. They spotted jelly fish, some gannets diving for fish and at one point a pod of dolphins came alongside and played in the wake of the boat before heading off into the distance. The boat remained in sight of the land all the way and Sam came to join them and started to point out some of the landmarks they could see. They had been fishing close to Lulworth Cove and as they headed for home Sam pointed out Durdle Door as they made their way towards Weymouth. At the mention of the name the boys went quiet, knowing the next time they crossed this stretch of water they would be on their journey home. As if on cue, Mick shouted from the cabin and pointed out to sea and there in the distance they could see a large passenger ship come into view heading towards Weymouth.

'That's the ferry from the Channel Islands coming back.' Sam said quietly. He had grown to love the boys and the realisation that they would be leaving, probably tomorrow, made him feel very sad.

Nothing more was said for quite a while until the few seagulls following them started to grow in number. There were a few bits of fish left in the buckets so the boys, egged on by Sam, started to throw the bits to the birds who started squawking loudly and fighting for the bits of food on offer.

Soon they were slowing down and approaching the dinghy. The sun had started to go down and it glistened on the wavelets as they drifted to a halt, creating a wonderful image that they would never forget. The seagulls realising there would be no more food had disappeared apart for one bird which had landed on the water and sat there patiently waiting to see if anything else might be offered his way.

The boys had expected all the crabs to come ashore with them but instead Mick gave Sam a large chancre in a sack to take home and put the lobster and two crabs in a bucket. The rest were secured in the store pot and lowered over the side on its own buoy. Sam explained to the boys that by doing this the crabs would be kept fresh and healthy so Mick could use them or sell them another day.

There was no need to take the net back this time so there was a bit more room in the dinghy. Mick gave the boys the task of rowing back to the pier which proved hilarious. They zigzagged their way back to the pier accompanied by a lot of instruction and guidance from Mick who sat in the stern of the dinghy. By the end of the short trip they were rowing, almost in unison and the zigzag had settled down. In fact, the boys asked if they could row a bit more but Mick wanted to get back and sell his lobster, so they were soon tied up alongside the pier and making their way back up the steps. At the top the boys stopped to thank Mick for their day out and everyone shook hands. Sam had a quiet word with Mick about the ferry times as they left and soon the three of them were headed back to Sam's house.

When they got there Ruth was waiting and when Sam produced the chancre, she was delighted. Ruth immediately went out to the shed and soon had a fire going under a large metal basin, heating the water to cook the crab. Soon the smell of cooked crab was everywhere and 20 minutes after the crab went into the pot Ruth was fishing the crab back out declaring it was ready.

As it cooled, Ruth buttered slices of bread and Sam came back with a hammer to attack the claws. Soon they were enjoying a feast of fresh crab and bread and butter. Ruth made the boys crab sandwiches to enjoy and they all savoured the treat but underlying the good mood around the table was the knowledge that this was probably the last time they would enjoy an evening meal together because tomorrow the boys would be heading home to the Channel Islands.

Chapter Twelve

After tea the boys headed off to bed leaving Sam and Ruth to clear away the dishes and have a bit of time together. Once the dishes were done the couple moved into their small lounge and closed the door.

'Seems like you had a nice day with the boys?' Ruth asked Sam as they sat down with a cup of tea.

Sam smiled recalling their day out with Mick. 'It was amazing.'

They sipped their tea for a few moments, both deep in thought.

Ruth noticed tears forming in Sam's eyes and put her tea down to give him a hug.

'I know,' she whispered, 'it would be lovely to have children of our own to enjoy happy times with. I am sure it will happen one day. I guess the time just isn't right yet.'

Sam squeezed Ruth's hand and smiled. 'I wish I had your confidence.'

Ruth brushed the tear from Sam's eye and kissed him gently on the lips.

Ruth stood and held out her hands. 'Come on, let's go to bed. Maybe tonight's the night,' she said with a wink.

*****

The next morning the blue sky had gone and had been replaced by a solid bank of grey. The skies reflected the mood in the small house in Fortuneswell. Breakfast was a sombre affair as the four sat around the table eating boiled eggs and soldiers. Ruth tried to smile but it was difficult as they all knew they were on the clock, literally.

While the table was cleared, and the dishes were done the boys got themselves ready and gathered their few belongings around them.

'Sam checked the time of the boat yesterday and we need to get to the docks by 11am.' Ruth stated in a let's get this done tone. 'Let's get cracking.'

There was a tear in her eye but a smile on her face as Ruth busied herself getting her coat on and making sure Sam was ready. Although it was only just after 8am it was important that they go now to make sure they got there in plenty of time. There was a lot of sadness around, but the good news was that the boys would not be on their own as Ruth and Sam planned to go with them.

They were soon off on their journey making their way off Portland and on to the coastal path towards Weymouth which ran alongside the railway line between Wyke Regis and Weymouth. As soon as they were off the road the ball was thrown down and the two lads, with Sam joining in, were kicking the ball along the path. Ruth noticed that PC showed no sign of a limp. *Thank goodness*, she thought. She had been worried he had done some damage to his leg yesterday.

In the distance towards the south the grey sky was striped with blue as the weather threatened to improve. At least it wasn't windy, and the sea was flat which meant that their trip should be a calm one, but no-one was trying to think about that right now.

The boys would stop to pick a blackberry or two as they made their way along the path, but Ruth made sure they kept up the pace as they made their way towards the turning up to Rodwell. One enthusiastic kick saw the ball end up on the railway line. Harry ran to get the ball back, but Ruth grabbed his shoulder to stop him just as a train passed by, sounding its horn as a belated warning. After the train had gone, disappearing into a tunnel up ahead, Harry turned to Ruth and gave her a huge hug, bursting into tears.

'What will I do without you? Who will be there to save me when I do something stupid?' He sobbed and sobbed as Ruth held him tight.

PC meanwhile went to retrieve the ball, being careful to look both ways before venturing on to the track.

Ruth grabbed Harry's shoulders and pushed him out to arm's length. 'Look at me,' she said to the sobbing young teenager. 'Look at me!' She snapped to get his attention.

Harry looked up with eyes red from crying and stared into Ruth's eyes.

'You are an incredible young man Harry,' she began. 'You have a great friend here in PC, the war is over so you have a long life to look forward to and when you get home you will have family waiting and all of your school friends. They will help you when, and if, you do something stupid. You will meet a lovely young girl and you will grow up with her and she will hug you when you are down and smile with you when you are happy. You have all this to look forward to so let's not hear any more nonsense from you. Look after each other until you get home and you will be fine.'

Harry had stopped crying during the pep talk and Sam had stood with his arm around PC's shoulder while Ruth had been speaking. He gave PC a squeeze and a smile as Harry regained his composure.

'Best we get on, the clock is ticking.' Sam offered. They all agreed, and with that 'moment' over they carried on towards Weymouth. Soon the boys were kicking the ball along the road to Rodwell and Sam and Ruth trailed behind holding hands as they walked.

Once through the town it was full speed ahead for Weymouth and the docks. They could see the smokestack of the boat they were heading for well before they reached the port itself. A steady stream of smoke lifted into the sky as her engines were warmed up prior to sailing. They had just half an hour to spare as they reached the quay and the scene was a hive of activity, with horse and carts, trucks, cranes and people all milling around, vying for the observer's attention. The boys could barely remember the last time they were on a boat like this, that time was 5 years ago and they were leaving their homes as part of the evacuation of the Channel Islands. Now they were doing it all again, leaving their homes of the last 5 years and heading back to who knew what. They stood as a group for a while in stunned silence as the ship was loaded and people made their way up the gangplank.

After what seemed like ages PC asked the question both the boys were chewing on. 'What do we do now?'

'Guess we had better get you some tickets.'

The boys followed Ruth and Sam towards the small ticket office on the pier and got in the short queue for tickets. As they waited an American army jeep pulled up on the pier behind the ticket office. Sister Christine and Nurse Catherine in their finest dress uniforms got out, accompanied by Major Bill, again in full uniform. They walked around the kiosk and confronted the boys. 'Going somewhere?' Major Bill asked the stunned boys in his deep voice and strong American accent.

The four stepped out of the queue.

'You must be Ruth,' Sister Christine offered holding out her hand to Ruth. Ruth shook her hand with a smile.

The boys edged back from the small group of adults.

'What is all this?' PC asked carefully.

'We're not going back to the hospital.' Harry added. The boys looked at each other and turned to run towards the gangplank of the ship.

As they ran strong hands grabbed their arms and stopped them in their tracks.

'Hold on there,' another familiar voice added to their confusion. It was Bill from the farm, helped by Karl the jeep driver.

The boys looked around in a panic not sure what to do and saw other familiar faces. John and Norma were there as was George from the George Hotel, Bill's wife Jean was talking to Nurse Catherine, Philip and Leanne were holding hands and smiling at them and even Edith was there talking to Ruth and Sister Christine. They couldn't believe what they were seeing, nearly everyone they had met along the way was there on the docks alongside the boat.

'What's happening,' PC asked to no-one in particular.

Sister Christine stepped forward. 'Sorry for the surprise boys,' she offered with her biggest smile. 'Ruth telephoned me at the Hospital to tell me where you were and to let me know you were safe. We had tracked you down as far as Portland,' she pointed to Nurse Catherine, 'but we weren't sure where you were exactly until Ruth called.'

'Sorry,' Ruth said quietly grabbing the two boys. 'I thought it would be a nice surprise for you before you head home.'

The boys had calmed down a bit now but were getting very emotional.

Another voice, a strange one this time, joined the conversation. 'I guess I should take over from here.'

The boys turned around. In front of them was the very imposing figure of the Captain of the TSS Sambur. Captain Mowbray had been a Destroyer Captain in the First World War until his boat had been sunk by a U-Boat in 1917 though all his crew were saved. He had joined the Great Western Railway between the wars and had Captained the TSS Sambur until 1940. However, after she had been commandeered by the Royal Navy the top brass had considered him too old to go back into the senior service. Not wanting to be left out of all the action he signed up for the Merchant Navy and had taken several ships across the Atlantic in the latter part of the war. He had seen terrible things and that combined with his sun wrinkled skin and rapidly greying hair looked a little older than his actual age of 66.

He gave the boys a salute and took off his cap and tucked it under his left arm. He shook the boy's hands in turn and then nodded to everyone else in the assembled party.

Once again turning to the boys he spoke gently. 'Your ship awaits.' He turned and pointed to the gangplank.

Harry and PC looked at each other and smiled. 'I suppose we had better go then,' PC said, looking around at group that surrounded them.

Edith came forward first and gave each of the boys a hug and everyone followed, hugging each of the boys in turn. Harry came to Norma last and they just looked at each other awkwardly. She looked at her Dad and he just nodded. She came forward and hugged Harry then gave him a kiss on the cheek. 'Don't forget me,' she whispered to him with a tear in her eye.

'I won't,' he replied bravely. 'I will see you again.'

While Harry was talking to Norma, PC got Sister Christine, Nurse Catherine, Bill and Jean and the Major to sign his football as they hadn't added their name to the ball during the journey.

Norma turned to PC and gave him a quick hug before the boys turned and followed the Captain up the gangplank on to the boat.

As soon as they were on the boat the gangplank was craned away and the ship prepared to get underway.

The three of them stood by the rail and the boys waved to the group below. The Captain asked them to stay on the deck until they were out of the harbour and pointed to some seats near the bow of the boat. Wait for me over there and I'll come back and see you once the ship has sailed.

With that the Captain saluted the group on the quay and made his way up to the bridge of his ship. With a wave from the bridge the ropes holding the ship to the quay in Weymouth were cast off and with a loud toot of its horn the ship pulled away and headed out of the harbour. The boys waved until they couldn't see the quay anymore and then sadly made their way towards the front of the boat.

Chapter Thirteen

PC and Harry sat down on a small wooden bench at the front of the boat and watched as they sailed out of Weymouth leaving England behind them.

As the landscape turned to a seascape and the gentle mist enveloped all sign of land PC looked down at his precious football that he now held on his lap. He slowly rotated it and remembered all the kind and generous people whose names were inscribed on the ball; some of the names were fading now but they would never fade from his mind.

The names started to blur as tears filled his eyes. They were finally on their way home.

He lent his head on to Harry's shoulder and his friend put his arm around his shoulder as PC gently sobbed.

Harry wanted to lift PC's mood but couldn't think of anything as the flat calm of the channel ahead offered little by way of a diversion.

Suddenly, as if to answer his prayers, there was a splash away to the left of the ship and a large fish broke the surface.

'PC look over there,' Harry said loudly. 'Dolphins!'

PC looked up and rubbed the tears from his eyes with his cuff. Soon several of the dolphins were racing alongside the boat and playing in the wake created by the ships bow.

The boys were soon engrossed watching the playful dolphins. Both were smiling broadly at the spectacle which nature was providing. The Captain came to join them to watch the dolphins and several of the passengers came to shake his hand and talk to him, mainly about the weather or the length of the journey ahead. Everyone seemed happy to be sailing to the

Islands. The Captain checked the boys were alright and they both nodded.

'I need to get back on the bridge to make sure we are going in the right direction,' the Captain said laughing with his eyes. 'I'll see you when we get nearer to home as it gets a bit rocky once we get near the islands.'

The Captain made his way back to the bridge and the dolphins disappeared as quickly as they had appeared. The boys sat back down and lulled by the throb of the engine and the gentle movement of the boat they both slept until a hubbub of excitement woke them. Over to the port side of the boat an Island was in clear view. They could also see a large lighthouse and the air was full of seabirds, gannets, just like the ones they had seen when they were on Mick's boat, except this time there seemed to be millions of them. The TSS Tambur was heading past Alderney and the Casquets lighthouse on its way towards Guernsey which was just visible in the distance off the starboard bow of the boat.

A member of the crew brought the boys a hot mug of cocoa, compliments of the Captain, and smiling, warmed by the cocoa and the sunshine they drew closer and closer to PC's home.

Then the reality struck them, this was the end of their journey together.

PC was the first to break the silence.

'When we split up, we'll keep in touch won't we?' PC asked Harry.

'Of course,' Harry replied instantly. 'We're blood brothers remember.'

'Blood brothers,' PC smiled, staring ahead at the growing mass of land which was his home.

I wonder what is waiting for me at home, he thought absently mindedly, trying to remember his family and also thinking of Glynis, his second mum back in Taunton. He looked again at the ball, remembering all the wonderful people that had helped them to get where they were now.

He looked up and he could start to make out details on the Island. The plume of smoke from the ship pointed away towards France so his view was as clear as it could be which allowed him to see the trees of Delancey park and the Vale Castle, two places he had visited often. He pondered what looked different and realised the large column on Delancey park had gone and over to his right, near L'Ancresse Common, he could make out a large tower that wasn't there before the Occupation.

He mentioned this to Harry, as they stood together looking across at the Island. Harry had never visited Guernsey so was fascinated to hear PC talk about all the places he remembered.

Harry's mind then turned to what he would find when he got home and who, if anyone, would be waiting for him.

Those thoughts were soon dismissed as PC spotted his house in the distance and excitedly pointed out the little harbour where he used to swim. There were some vehicles on the road, and they could see the occasional bus heading along the front as PC called the main coastal road between St Peter Port and St Sampsons. There were also quite a few trucks on the road and PC wondered if tomato exports had started already.

The cranes around the port dominated the harbour scene, as did Castle Cornet which had protected St Peter Port from invaders for hundreds of years. There was a large freighter in the harbour being unloaded, no doubt with much needed supplies for the Islanders, also a small naval vessel flying the White Ensign. It seemed to stand out against the largely grey background comprised of granite walls and unpainted concrete.

PC went quiet as the ferry turned into the harbour and the dilapidated nature of the view came ever closer. He began to realise the Island was nothing like the one he had left five years ago.

It would be a long time before the Island returned to normal, he thought to himself.

Harry was quiet too as he knew this was the moment he was dreading. His one real friend in life was about to head back to his family leaving him on his own and he was convinced there would be no-one to welcome him when he eventually arrived back in Jersey, which was now visible as a low land mass in the distance.

The ferry was now maneuvering itself against the jetty with lines being thrown ashore and collected by willing stevedores on the quayside. There were a few people on the pier waving up at people on the boat and passengers were now gathered around the boys waving back. PC didn't recognise anyone and felt a bit deflated. He had imagined that his mum and dad would have somehow known he was coming back and would be there waiting for him.

Some of the seasoned travellers were already heading towards where the gangway would be placed and soon the boys were on their own as the mass of people waited to head ashore.

The Captain suddenly appeared and took off his cap as he approached them.

'Well boys, this is Guernsey and it's time for Peter to head home. Do you want to say your goodbyes and I'll escort you off my ship,' he said, turning towards PC?

'Thank you, sir,' PC replied quietly, turning towards Harry.

He turned to his friend and dropped his bag and the ball and gave Harry a huge hug. The Captain stooped and picked up the ball as it started to roll away, noting the names written on its battered surface.

‘Thank you for being my friend and for everything, I’ll never forget you and you will always be my brother,’ he blurted out as the tears started to flow again.

‘Come on son,’ the Captain said to PC. ‘I need to get Harry home too.’

He had watched the boys from the bridge for most of the journey and knew how hard this moment was for them.

PC eventually let Harry go and turned to go with the Captain. He picked up his bag and took the ball from the Captain. Then after taking a few steps away he suddenly turned and ran back to Harry.

‘Here, take the ball Harry, that way you’ll always remember me and this adventure.’ He thrust out his arms with the ball which Harry took after a moment’s hesitation.

‘Thanks PC, thank you so much. I will treasure it.’ Harry smiled at his friend and tears filled his eyes too as PC turned away and was guided towards the gangway by the Captain.

He watched as PC went down on to the jetty where suddenly out of the shadows a man and woman appeared. He knew instantly who they were and smiled as PC suddenly noticed them and ran from the Captain into the embrace of his mum and dad.

After offering a few words to the family, the Captain saluted them and made his way back up the gangway as the few passengers travelling from Guernsey to Jersey started to make their way on to the ship behind him.

He came back and stood with Harry and watched as Peter pointed to Harry and they all waved up to him.

Harry smiled and waved back.

The Captain looked down at the tear streaked face of the boy next to him and had an idea.

'Harry, would you like to steer the ship back to Jersey?'

Harry looked up at him. 'Yes please,' he said, amazed at the offer.

'Come on then, let me show you up to the bridge.'

With a final wave to PC and his parents, Harry followed the Captain through a door marked crew only and up on to the bridge of the ship. The precious ball tucked under his arm.

The Captain asked one of the crew on the bridge to give Harry his cap and showed him the wheel.

'Once we get out of the harbour Harry, I want you to take the wheel. I'll tell you which way to go and then you can steer us home.

'Thanks Captain, I think I know my way,'

The Captain laughed. 'We'll see son, we'll see.'

Harry looked back down to the jetty as PC, with his parent either side of him walked out of sight on their way home. He wished the same welcome would be waiting for him but knew that wasn't going to happen.

Soon after more passengers had come on board and some crates had been off loaded by the cranes, the Captain asked Harry to pull a toggle. When he pulled the toggle, the ships horn sounded, loud over his head. He almost jumped out of skin. 'Give it two more Harry,' the skipper ordered and with that the ropes were cast off and they were on their way to

Jersey. Harry looked back at the jetty just in time to see PC run back around the buildings and wave like crazy at the boat as it moved. He moved to the edge of the bridge and waved back.

'Bye PC,' he shouted. 'See you soon.'

PC was shouting too but with all the noise they couldn't here each other. As the boat reversed out PC ran to the end of the Jetty and waved and waved until the boat left the harbour and his parents had come back to fetch him. They stayed until the boat passed the lighthouse at the end of the castle walk and then turned for home.

Harry heard the Captain cough. 'I hope you are not failing on your duties young man,' he said with a smile.

'No sir,' Harry replied heading back to the wheel and taking over from the helmsman. 'Which way?'

'I thought you knew the way,' the Captain said smiling as he pointed towards Jersey. 'That way, let's get you home.'

With that the Captain called for full ahead and the bells rang as the instruction was fed to the engine room. Almost instantly the ship leapt forward, and they were on their way to Jersey.

The 26 miles home seemed to fly by for Harry as the bridge was a hive of activity during the voyage. More hot chocolate was passed around and everyone kept a look out for any debris in the water, other ships or small boats. There were still worries about the occasional floating mine, so the lookouts were on high alert. By now the day was almost past as the sun began to sink in the west.

Once the ship reached the Corbiere Lighthouse, which stood proud on the south western tip of the Island, he was shown where to steer the ship as it headed towards Elizabeth Castle and St Helier. He could make out a large tower on the Corbiere Headland that hadn't been their when he left 5 years ago. He suddenly wished PC had been there so he could tell him all about Jersey. I'll invite him over one day, he thought to himself.

Soon the helmsman had to take over as they made their approach to the harbour of St Helier.

The same docking process as he had witnessed in Guernsey was soon taking place as the ship came alongside the quay. People were waiting for the ship to dock as she would be making her way back to England after a short stay on the Island. There were also people waiting to greet the passengers who were already waiting to climb down the gangway. Harry didn't recognise anyone on the quay from his position on the bridge.

'Come on son,' the Captain said. 'Let's get you ashore.'

Almost reluctantly Harry grabbed his bag and the cherished ball and made his way down to the gangway. It was almost clear now as the last of the passengers made their way down on to the quay and dispersed.

The Captain guided Harry down the gangway and then stopped at the bottom. He stayed on the gangway as Harry stepped down.

'How did you like steering the boat son?' The Captain asked.

Harry turned and smiled. 'It was fantastic thank you.'

'Maybe you should train to join the merchant navy,' the Captain suggested.

'I think I would like that, especially when the sea is flat like it was today, but what's it like in rough weather?' Harry asked.

'She rolls like a barrel,' the Captain laughed.

‘What do I do now?’ Harry asked.

‘I’m not sure Harry, why don’t you ask this chap?’

Harry, looking puzzled turned around and there with his arms open wide was his Dad.

‘DAD!!’ Harry almost screamed and, dropping everything, ran into his father’s arms. ‘How… I thought you were dead,’ Harry stammered, tears of joy running down his face.

‘The Germans caught me, and I have been locked away in a prisoner of war camp ever since. I’ve only just been repatriated.’

Not for the first time the Captain picked up the treasured football and came up to join the father and son.

‘Did you know sir?’ Harry asked the Captain.

‘Yes, I had a message before we left Weymouth so I knew your father would be waiting for you. I thought it would be a nice surprise,’ he added offering the ball back to Harry who took it gratefully, tucking it under his arm.

‘What’s that,’ his Dad asked him.

‘It belongs to my best friend,’ Harry said. ‘I’ll explain when we get home. We do have a home?’ He added.

‘Oh yes,’ his Dad replied, ‘and you have your own room waiting for you.’

‘Oh, and these guys wanted to say hello too.’ With that a bunch of his old school friends ran out from behind a shed on the dock. ‘Harry!’ They all shouted as they ran over to meet him.

Harry was beaming from ear to ear.

His Dad walked over to the Captain leaving Harry with his friends. ‘Thank you, Captain,’ Harry’s Dad offered his hand. ‘I can’t say just how much I appreciate all of this.’

The Captain shook his hand.

‘My pleasure, I hope the boys get to meet up again one day, but I’ll let Harry tell you his story. Have a great life and let’s hope we don’t have to go through a war like that again.’

‘Let’s hope not.’

The Captain saluted, as he had in Guernsey, and walked back up the gangway to his ship.

The boys and Harry’s Dad turned to leave the quay. As they walked away Harry turned and waved back to the Captain one last time. As they walked, he looked at the ball and there in fresh ink was the Captain’s signature and the ships name ,TSS Sambur.

He smiled and with his Dad’s arm around his shoulder walked home, surrounded by his friends. His adventure was over, and he had an exciting life to look forward to, with his Dad.

Chapter Fourteen

Springfield, Jersey 1954

With a roar from the capacity crowd the two teams walked out on the pitch, resplendent in their red and white and green and white colours and began to warm up. The referee carried the ball to the centre circle, placed it on the spot and called the Captains across to toss the coin and choose halves. The Jersey skipper came across with his pennant and the Guernsey Captain jogged across to join the group in the centre circle. He too carried his pennant, they shook hands, then exchanged pennants.

Guernsey won the toss and chose to play with the wind behind them. The Jersey skipper, Harold "Harry" Le Maistre, shook the referee's hand but before he could turn to run back to his half, the Guernsey Captain called out to him above the roar of the crowd.

'I think there is someone you would like to meet Harry,' the Guernsey Captain shouted.

He turned and waved to the players warming up and one of them broke away and headed over to the circle.

Harry looked hard at the approaching player who didn't stop for a handshake, instead he threw his arms around the startled Jersey skipper, much to the amusement of the referee and the Guernsey Captain.

'Wotcha Harry, long time no see.'

Harry was totally shocked.

'PC! Is that you?'

He returned the hug and looking back all the Guernsey players were standing and watching, many applauding as the two old friends met again for the first time in nearly ten years.

'We'll catch up after the game Harry,' PC suggested before running back. He turned as he ran. 'Good Luck Harry, you'll need it,' PC laughed.

Harry shouted back. 'Good Luck to you too!'

Soon the teams were lining up and the referee blew his whistle. Guernsey kicked off and for the next ninety minutes friendships were put on hold as both teams battled to win what would be one of the most epic games in Muratti history.

During the next 90 minutes the game ebbed and flowed and PC stood out, bagging two goals in each half with the final result going in favour of Guernsey 5 - 3. The Guernsey fans were ecstatic and some of the supporters ran on to the pitch and carried PC off on their shoulders, the hero of the hour. Even the Jersey fans applauded what had been an outstanding match and a wonderful individual performance.

In the post-match melee Harry didn't get the chance to see PC and decided to wait until after they had all got cleaned up and met up for the post-match celebrations and commiserations.

When they were all together Harry looked around the reception room for PC as the players and officials enjoyed drinks together and relived the match and shared tales of the chances that got away. However, he couldn't see PC anywhere. In the end he spotted the Guernsey skipper and asked him where Harry was.

'Didn't you know? PC has just become a father and he is going home on the Isle of Sark with the Lieutenant Governor so he can be with his wife and son.'

'Damn,' Harry exclaimed. 'I wanted to see him before he left.'

Harry went to find the team Manager and then popped to see the referee before calling a taxi.

'The Harbour please mate,' he told the driver and off they sped from Springfield down to the seafront.

At the docks the area around the Isle of Sark was a riot of green and white as some of the Guernsey fans were getting on board to make their way home. He pushed his way through the throng but then caught site of a commotion up on the Bridge. There, with the Lieutenant Governor, was PC, waving to the fans. A cheer went up and PC smiled back, holding the trophy aloft.

As the fans quietened down Harry shouted at the top of his voice. 'PC, PC!'

PC heard him and looked down to see Harry waving.

He turned to the Captain of the boat and left him with the trophy and made his way down to the gangplank. The crowd parted when they saw him, and he was soon down on the quay and shaking Harry's hand.

'Well done PC, I couldn't stop you this time eh!' Harry smiled.

'Not this time,' PC replied. 'Glad I've still got two goods legs eh!'

They laughed.

'I've got you something.' Harry said, pulling out the match ball from behind his back. 'I got a few of the lads to sign it and I have written my address on it too so you can get in touch.'

'Don't be a stranger,' he added. 'I would love you to meet the wife. Do you remember Norma?'

'From Chard, of course I do.' PC beamed. 'You sly dog!'

‘Got a baby on the way too!’

‘I have a boy too, just a week old which is why they are letting me go home. Sorry I couldn’t see you after the game. They rushed me out of the dressing room to make sure I got on the boat.’

‘Thanks for the ball Harry, it will replace the one I gave you all those years ago.’ PC added.

‘I’ve still got that ball,’ Harry said with a tear in his eye. ‘They were good days.’

‘They sure were.’

The wail of the steamer’s horn broke the moment as the two old friends, were suddenly overwhelmed with the memories of the days they spent in 1945, kicking that football as they made their way home on a journey that would be a special part of their lives forever. An adventure which was so rare and exciting that they would always remember those days and cherish them until their dying day.

‘Got to go,’ said PC. ‘My wife and our baby are waiting for me.’

‘Travel safe,’ said Harry, ‘can I come over and see you? Maybe in the summer.’

‘Of course, I’ll get in touch once everything has settled down and we can set a date.’

They gave each other a big hug and PC dropped the ball. It started rolling towards the gap between the quay and the boat, but Harry was quick. He ran after it, trapped the ball under his feet and flipped it up on to his knee, swiveled and passed the ball into PC’s hands in one smooth movement.

PC smiled. 'Still got the tricks eh Harry.'

'Oh yes,' he replied. 'Hope you'll see more in next year's Muratti.'

'I'll see you before then.' We'll have a kick about when you come over.'

With that he ran up the gangplank just as the stevedores were getting ready to remove it and disappeared into the ship. Next thing he was back up on the ships bridge and waving down at Harry. He reached down and lifted up the trophy as if to taunt Harry who laughed back at him.

'I'll get that back next year,' Harry shouted up at PC. The ship's horn sounded three times and the lines were cast off. Slowly the ship pulled away from the quay and headed out of the harbour. Harry could see PC waving all the way until the ship was too far away to make him out on the bridge.

Harry walked back to the end of the quay and managed to get a taxi back to Springfield to catch up with the rest of his team. There would be a Muratti Ball and big celebratory meal that evening and he and Norma would be attending along with the rest of his teammates and the Guernsey team, less PC of course.

The match had been broadcast on the Home Service with the famous John Arlott providing the commentary, so the score was widely known on Guernsey. As a result, that evening, it was estimated that 10,000 Islanders were waiting at St Peter Port harbour to welcome PC and the Lieutenant Governor home. He stood on the bridge of the ship waving to the crowd as the Isle of Sark docked. The Guernsey fans from the boat added themselves to the throng as a sea of green and white wearing Islanders struggled to get a glimpse of their new hero. Someone started singing Sarnia Cherie, the Islanders national song, and soon everyone else joined in, creating scenes reminiscent of the Liberation in 1945.

PC went straight from the harbour, after battling his way through the crowds, to the Maternity Hospital where his wife was waiting for him with their new baby son. Everyone in the ward applauded as he came in and he proudly held his son up high, as if he was the Muratti Vase he had held aloft at Springfield, just a few hours before.

That summer Harry and Norma visited Guernsey and met PC and his family and had a great week together touring the Island and reminiscing about their time in Taunton and how they had made their way home with the ball in the summer of 1945. It would be a friendship that would last a lifetime.

The End

Epilogue

Some of you that know Guernsey Muratti history will recognise that the 1954 Muratti was a 5 - 3 win for Guernsey at Springfield and the hero that day was my father Micky Brassell. The story of that match is part of Muratti legend and the bit about the baby being born reflected how I was carried around the maternity hospital in triumph when the news broke of the win.

I have, and treasure, the medal that was given to my Dad that day which he had engraved and gave to me for my birthday one year. If I recall right it may have been my 40th.

Dad played football until a knee injury cut his career short and by the early 60's his career was over. He won three Muratti caps, two wins and one loss but never scored again. After football was over, he took up golf and played that until walking became an issue. Now his memory is fading but where he sits is a treasured copy of the History of the Muratti and he reads and re-reads the story of the 1954 final as if ensuring it is a time he will never forget.

Dad told me of his time in Taunton and recently out of the blue I received a copy of a letter his Dad had sent a friend when he was in the army. In the letter he talked about how my Dad captained his school team in Swanage at the tender age of 9, showing his prowess at the game at such an early age. His father, my grandfather was also a Muratti player.

The story is complete fiction but was inspired by the story of the evacuation and my father's dedication to the game he loved.

He was friends with dozens of fellow footballers for years, many of them joining him on the golf course as their careers ended and I know he knew many Jersey footballers too.

Harry Le Maistre was inspired by the great Jersey player, Graeme Le Maistre and PC is a reference to a schoolboy friend and teammate of mine, Richard Cochrane, who sadly died too soon.

Acknowledgement and Thanks

I would like to thank my wife who was happy for me to spend some of our precious holiday time driving the route the boys took between Taunton and Portland Bill.

I had never been to Taunton before and thinking that my Dad may have walked the same roads during the war was quite moving for me. The scenery of the area and the lovely towns along the way were inspiring. Chesil Beach was particularly impressive, and I just wished I had taken the time to visit the swannery at Abbotsbury.

If anyone is thinking of visiting the area, I would highly recommend it, just give yourself more time than we had.

As usual the computer has been a source of a lot of information with Google Maps and Wikipedia in particular being prime sources of research when needed.

I would also like to thank everyone who encouraged me along the way into writing this second book and to my wife who will also be proof reading this one for me. As a nurse, she was the inspiration for Sister Christine.

As I type the coronavirus is rife in the country and I guess in a strange way it has given me the motivation to get this book finished and the time for me to start my third book.

This is my second novel, the first being Ten Days One Guernsey Summer. If you haven't read that one yet please do.

The working title for the third book is - The Battle for Guernsey.

Thank you for reading this book and for your support.

Keep safe.

About the Author

I started writing Journey Home as soon as I finished my first novel, Ten Days One Guernsey Summer, in the summer of 2017. It was dedicated to a certain extent to my father who after spending much of the war in the south west of England, came back to Guernsey and became one of the best known Muratti footballers in the history of Guernsey football. That was due to his performance in the 1954 Muratti final when he scored 4 goals in a 5 - 3 victory in Jersey. It came to be known as Brassell's Muratti.

I was just a few days old when that match took place and he was given leave to come back on the boat that evening to see Mum and me, with hundreds of the Guernsey supporters who had made the day trip. He was even allowed to bring the trophy back with him. He was met at the harbour by a crowd which was estimated to be 10,000 strong, such was the interest in the sport and the achievement of that great man.

From then on, I was to be Micky Brassell's son and have lived with that honour, in the Island of my birth all my life. I spent a long career in the Civil Service, acquiring a wide knowledge of Guernsey and have a keen interest in the Island's heritage and culture, in a wide range of areas.

For many years I was known as the Island's native guide, within the Civil Service, and have escorted VIP's at the highest level, including a Deputy Prime Minister, when they have visited Guernsey.

When I left the Civil Service, I established a local tour company called Experience Guernsey Limited and operated that business until 2008. In 2007 I also became a business advisor with the Guernsey Enterprise Agency, trading as Startup Guernsey, helping people to get started in business. That ended with the closure of the Agency in December of 2019. I was also the Branch Office for the IoD Guernsey Branch from 2012 to December 2019.

I build, host, and maintain websites for businesses and private individuals through the domain www.newebsites.co.uk and in the spare time I have left I love to write and am planning on getting back into my painting.

My unique perspective on Guernsey, through a lifetime based on the Island, and from a family who were evacuated, inspired me to write Ten Days One Guernsey Summer and this book seemed the perfect follow up to that first novel. I have now moved with my wife to Sunderland and hopefully will have more time to write.

Please remember Journey Home is a complete work of fiction. The Islands of Jersey and Guernsey have always had a healthy rivalry on the sporting field and in the field of business. However this story was designed to show that despite all of that, we are united in the face of any adversity and will work together when needed to overcome all odds and in truth are the closest of friends when battles on the field of sport are over.

I hope you enjoyed this book. I am off to work on the next one. Look out for 'The Battle for Guernsey' on Amazon.

Cheers.

Tony Brassell

Chris and Tony Brassell